Soccer Books for Kids 8-12: The Most Powerful Soccer Stories of All Time for Young Soccer Fans

Chest Dugger

Contents

ABOUT THE AUTHOR

Chest Dugger is a soccer fan, former professional and coach. He is fascinated by the mental side of sport, as well as the physical. Enjoy this book and several others that he has written.

Disclaimer

Free Gift Included

As part of our dedication to help you improve your soccer game, we have sent you a free soccer drills worksheet, known as the "Soccer Training Work Sheet" drill sheet. The worksheet is a list of drills that you can use to improve your game and a methodology to track your performance on these drills on a day-to-day basis. We want to get you to the next level.

Click on the link below to get your free drills worksheet.

https://soccertrainingabiprod.gr8.com/

Introduction: The Mindset of Masters

Who is the number one soccer player of all time? Which players should make the top ten of any list? Questions to spark debate in every home, every bar and at every ground. This book will offer some suggestions – some unquestionable, others perhaps a little more controversial. More than that, we will explore what has sent these greats to the top of the sporting world's biggest tree, and whether there are any common themes among the lifts and hoists they used to get themselves there.

Because there must be something that turns the very good into the brilliant, the top international into the best there is. Or, as with our players here, the best there has ever been. One reason for their success will be physical, without doubt. You cannot become a top performer in any sport without being extremely good at it. But there is something about the mindset of people who reach the very top. Something that sets them apart. That is true of any field, not just the soccer world, or even the wider sporting community. And if we can identify the nature of that mysterious attribute, maybe we can call on it ourselves.

Soccer is without doubt the most popular sport on the planet. It is played from Brazil to Burundi, from Egypt to England, from France to the Faroe Islands. It is growing rapidly as a participation sport in the US, and the development of the women's game is making it truly inclusive. It is played to all standards and at all levels, from the Under sixes starting out in organized matches, to the vets' teams and walking soccer enjoyed by players who are, we might say, looking over their shoulder back towards their prime. It is played with keepie uppies in the backyard, through to kick arounds in the park, in playgrounds and school matches, through clubs and the semi-pro game to the ultimate thrill of professional soccer played in front of tens of thousands of fans. At its absolute best the sport is celebrated in the finals of the European Cup, the Copa America, the European Championships and the World Cup.

The joy of soccer is that it requires almost nothing in order to play. Two shirts as goalposts and a ball. Or even, as we will discover in the pages ahead, a ball substitute. Rolled up paper in a sock, even a melon or some rags tied into a bundle. It is also the ideal spectator sport. Mankind's tribal instincts are satisfied by it; the atmosphere of a packed stadium is hard to beat. The game manages to get the frequency of its major purpose – scoring goals – about right. Enough to hold the watcher's interest, but not so many that scoring ever loses its absolute thrill…for player as well as fan.

And of course, at the epitome of the world's love for soccer are two elements. The club (or international team) who fans support and the star names who represent that team. This book will look at ten of the finest players of the game to ever grace a soccer field. The stars who light up the pitch. Whose names are chanted on the terraces and whose legacies continue to shape the game and will do so for years to come. In looking at the careers of these players, this book will seek to delve into their past. To look at their formative years in the game to identify what it is that creates the best. Naturally, athleticism, skill, technique and commitment are all to the fore, but we will consider exactly what factors help to create the mindset that turns a fine athlete and very good practitioner into a truly global star, one whose reputation stands the test of time.

Not everyone will agree that our collection is the right one. But few will question that every player we have selected is up there with the best. Our choices include the great Brazilian, Pele. The player who lit up the 1970 World Cup, the shining star of the brilliant Brazil teams of an era which stretched from the late 1950 to those finals in Mexico. The man who many consider to be the greatest of all time. We will examine the career of Ferenc Puskas, the player who seemed to possess a physique diametrically opposed to that we associate with great sports players. One whose soccer journey was curtailed and almost ended by the intervention of politics but who had the strength of character to make a decision which changed his life forever.

We will consider the Dutch maestro Johann Cruyff, a man whose legacy shaped the game in its current form and who put back the 'beautiful' in the Beautiful Game, just when it seemed as though expediency and defensive strength would define the future of soccer, in its turn squeezing the excitement out of the sport. Draining the lifeblood on which fans thrive. Without Cruyff, the possibility exists that soccer today would be looking upwards to the apex of the sporting tree, rather than sitting atop it, viewing the progress of other sports as they try to emulate its ideal mixture of excitement, skill, passion and uncertainty.

Fans of today are fortunate to be blessed by not one but two of the greatest players of all time. Lionel Messi and Cristiano Ronaldo have dominated the game for a decade and a half. And although age is catching up with both, it seems not to slow them down. Each remains a leading global performer well into their thirties.

We will consider the greatest player in the one position on the park where most must wait until their thirties to reach their peak. The goalkeeper. Peter Schmeichel was for years the best keeper on the planet, helping Manchester United to long lasting glory and even being a part of one the biggest ever shocks of European International football, keeping the Danish goal secure as tiny Denmark, home to just five million people, won the 1992 European championships.

Staying with the defense, we will spend some time looking at the factors which made Bobby Moore perhaps the greatest defender of all time; a player who redefined the role of the center back and whose talents as a ball player were years ahead of their time. These days, a center half is much more than a stopper, and is often the player who begins attacks which lead to scoring opportunities. This type of player can trace their roots back to the magnificent boots of Bobby Moore.

In order to be considered the best, it appears as though a successful international career is required as well as brilliant club achievements. But what if a player happens to be born outside of a major soccer playing nation? Such a fate befell George Best. Northern Ireland is a principality which adores soccer but with a population of just a million and a half, it is never going to be a world power in the game. George Best had his demons, as we shall see, but his talent on the pitch was second to very few indeed.

Zinedine Zidane's career came during a period of French dominance in world soccer. He is a man who might end being remembered for a moment of (justified?) madness when he headbutted Marco Materazzi after the Italian was abusive about his sister during the 2006 World Cup final. But that should not be the case. Because Zidane was a master with the ball, delivering soccer retribution even more effectively than he delivered physical revenge on that fateful day.

There is one player who might justifiably claim to leave Best behind as a dribbler, and Zidane as a man who may have hit the self-destruct button in his final international match. He is also perhaps the only player whose talents truly challenge Pele's position as the greatest of all time. Another player who, like Best, had his troubles. And who, like the Irishmen, eventually paid the ultimate price for his off the field excesses. Another who, like Zidane this time, is remembered in some parts for his soccer playing misdemeanors as much as his genius. We refer, of course, to Diego Maradona. A man blessed with so much impish brilliance that he can claim to have scored both the most outrageous and the most wonderful World Cup goals in history. In the same match. We shall also see how Diego Maradona crossed the threshold between sporting icon and national deity. A remarkable feat considering, or maybe because of, his humble beginnings.

We also have Toni Adams, Gigi Buffon, Gerd Muller and Josef Bican to round out the list. There were more, of course, whom we could have included. Fans will have their own nominees for this book. Franz Beckenbauer in place of Bobby Moore? We have no full backs in the group, nor defensive midfielders. On the creative side, Michel Platini could easily have made the cut. There is no place for the vision and touch of the second greatest ever Dutch player, Dennis Bergkamp, or Ferenc Puskas' Real Madrid strike partner, Alberto Di Stefano. No room for the other Ronaldo, the Brazilian one. No space for the French genius, the always controversial Eric Cantona. We are conscious of a lack of players from the earliest days of the game, or even the era pre and immediately post second world war. The likes of Sir Stanley Matthews do not make the cut, even though Matthews was still playing top class football at the age of fifty. He was also the man who won the very first Ballon d'Or…when he was 41 years old!

All, and many others, could have been a part of our story. But in the pages ahead we will seek to find patterns and consistency in the make-up of these greats, and in doing so, maybe even help towards the identification of the players who might in future join this list of ten of the finest footballers (soccer players) to feature in the history of the sport. Because, as we shall see, the genius of the very best lays not only in their boots, but in their minds as well. And, even, in some less tangible influences on their career.

Bullied but the Greatest

We must start with the greatest of them all. Although, it is only by chance that the great man carries the name **Pele**. It is widely known that the Brazilian was first named Edson Arantes do Nascimento - apparently the Edson bit is a derivation of Edison, after Thomas Edison. This lightbulb moment perhaps suggests that soccer was not the intended path Dondinho and Celeste Arantes wanted their eldest son to follow.

However, it was soon apparent that the kid was special. Dondinho was a fine soccer player himself and was renowned for his bravery on the pitch. So, Pele was, first of all, 'Dico', which means 'Son of a Warrior.' Pele came later, from his peers at school and was maybe not a name with which he wanted to be associated, at least as a youngster.

Young Edson carried a small speech defect, and kids can be cruel beasts. The goalkeeper of the local soccer team, Vasco da Gama, was Bile. But Pele could not pronounce his 'b' sound. From his childish mouth Bile became Pile, and that made his even more puerile classmates tease him, and refer to him as 'Pele'.

As a child, Pele was admired for his calmness under stress and his tolerance. Victims of bullying can go one of three ways. They can internalize their pain and become withdrawn. They can lash out in anger, drawing more derision from their peers. Or they can accept and move forwards. From a young age, Pele was blessed with two of the characteristics essential in a top-class sports player. He had the genes of a fighter, a winner. And these were tempered by a personality that remained calm under pressure. But a great must also have a trigger point; he or she must possess the passion to lift them in times of crisis. The youngster had this in abundance. It was the characteristic which would later serve him so well on the world stage. Kicked and hacked half to death by defenders not fit to wash his boots, he had the emotional strength not to react, and get himself sent off the pitch. But this was allied to a fortitude which made him take revenge on his opponents, and to exact it in the most effective way possible. By destroying them with the ball.

This mental strength was something he carried with him into adulthood and the most astonishing of playing careers. Pele broke into the Santos first team at the age of just fifteen. Even more remarkably, he was representing his nation a year later. It was in the 1958 World Cup that he announced himself to the world. At that time, he was the youngest player to represent any nation in the finals and became the star of the tournament. The greatest players have the ability to perform on the biggest occasions. Pele had that talent in abundance. He scored the winner in the quarter finals against Wales, then bagged a second half hat trick against France in the semis.

It was a tournament where underdogs thrived (although Brazil cannot be included in that category). The final saw hosts Sweden take on the South Americans, and once more it was their teenage sensation who dominated. Brazil ran out relatively easy winners that day, beating the Scandinavians 5-2. Pele once more scored – this time netting twice. Sigvard Parling was a member of that Sweden team which did so well in the competition, but even he admitted to admiring the genius that was, is, Pele. 'When Pele scored the fifth goal in that Final, I have to be honest and say I felt like applauding,' he later said.

Of course, soccer in the sixties was a hard game. The 1962 tournament should have seen Brazil, the best team there by miles, celebrating the magic of the round ball. Instead, the finals were a disgrace of violent tactics and obscene tackling. They took place in Chile, and the most famous match was the one which became known as the Battle of Santiago, as the Chileans and Italians kicked and punched lumps out of each other. It was a playground brawl, with recalcitrant kids smacking each other behind the teacher's back, as he tried desperately to maintain some kind of order. There are some great clips on YouTube, including the best, introduced by the well-known commentator David Coleman, where he disregards the BBC rule of not expressing an opinion on events, such is his understated outrage at the course of the match. Remind yourself, as you watch, that this is not a boxing fight, nor is it footage of the sort of hooliganism which ruled European football – especially English, Dutch and Italian – during the 1970s and 1980s. It is soccer. At the highest level. Except, what we watch is not soccer.

The other event of any note of that tournament was the determination of opponents to kick Pele out of it. If you cannot match his skill, and nobody could, then opponents' philosophy appeared to be stop him playing. The second rate succeeded in their aim, and the greatest player of all time appeared in only two matches before opponent-induced injury took him out of the competition. Although Brazil went on to retain their title as champions, that they had to do so without their star player is both an indictment on the competition, and a commendation of their talents.

It was widely assumed that they would repeat their feat in 1966, but another rising star who could easily have appeared among our list of greats knocked them out. The Portuguese Eusebio was in his prime and contributed to a 3-1 victory over the defending champions which saw them fail to progress. By 1970, in Mexico, the Brazilians were once more top of the tree. Pele was by now approaching the twilight of his magnificent career, but he was still good enough to score four goals in the competition, dominate the final (a 4-1 victory over Italy) and win the Golden Ball, the award given to the tournament's best player.

So, three World Cups out of four for the Brazilians, and their maestro conducted them to victory in two of them, as well as playing a big part in the other before being forced out of the competition. Pele famously finished his career by playing in the new and promising US football league, along with many of the greats of their day. He joined New York Cosmos for a reputed $7 million in 1975 and led them to the US title. He also committed himself to promoting the game in the US and can be credited for laying the foundations of the game there today. His final match was in 1977, and he played one half for his current team, NY Cosmos, and the other for Santos. In 1999, he was named Athlete of the Century by the International Olympic Committee. Not just the best soccer player, but the greatest sports player of the century.

All that and consider that Pele was, his US excursion apart, a one club man. He represented Santos throughout his career. He never played in Europe, he was in his prime during the days when soccer on TV was largely limited to the World Cup, domestic and European competitions in most of the world. He was subject to nothing like the exposure of many of the other players in this list. Yet still he is widely regarded as the best of the best.

There is perhaps a sad note on which to conclude his sporting career. At the age of 75, the greatest footballer the world has seen was due to have his enduring brilliance celebrated as he performed an iconic event. Lighting the cauldron at the 2016 Rio Olympics. But 75 at the time, the player was recovering from hip surgery, and his doctors advised against him attempting to reach the cauldron. The sight of him being winched up in a wheelchair was considered to be too traumatic, and the star made the final decision to withdraw. Probably that was a wise decision, best to remember the great man in his prime.

But all that was to come. As a young boy Pele was yet to develop the strength of purpose to defeat a foe with skill, and like most kids, when pushed too far, he reacted with his voice and his fists. Usually, words were as far as he went, but the other children saw that calling him 'Pele' got the reaction they wanted, and so they did it more. Sometimes, they went too far. Pele was once suspended from school for two days for hitting out. The innocent victim receiving the punishment.

It is hard to see the greatest exponent of the greatest sport the world has ever witnessed – in both cases – as a victim of childhood bullying. But he was.

'It was not a nickname I wanted as a child,' the great man once said of the name 'Pele'. 'My family called me Dico, my mates in the street called me Edson.' But ultimately, that sense of serenity which would later make it appear as though he had all the time in the world on the soccer pitch took precedence over his anger.

'Then I realized it wasn't up to me what I'm called. Now I love the name – but back then it wound me up no end,' he said. You cannot beat a person who does not recognize defeat.

Of course, students of the game – or students of theology (not that these are mutually exclusive groups) will know that serendipitously the name Pele could not be more appropriate for a man blessed with brilliance in his feet. The name exists in the bible no less and is the Hebrew for miracle. Those fortunate enough to ever see the maestro play in the flesh will know that such a term employs no hyperbole when applied to the man.

We can see already in the anecdote above the mental acuity and strength of character, the willingness to learn and the self-confidence which would shape the man, and which played such an essential role in him becoming a great. The world, though, was close to missing out on finding its greatest ever player. It just goes to show how chance plays such a role in life. Because Pele's dream was to achieve the heights not on a soccer pitch but literally in the skies. He wanted to become a pilot. The story goes that the determined young lad was committed to this career until a light plane crashed near his home. The boy took himself to the local hospital, presumably to wish his hero well, and instead discovered a mangled corpse. The shock played its part, and his dream of becoming a pilot faded. We cannot call that accident serendipitous – there was certainly nothing happy about it for the pilot who lost his life, or his family and friends – but it did have the silver lining of turning Pele's head away from the stars and down to the green fields of the world of soccer.

Actually, that Pele dreamed for a while of becoming a pilot is evidence of another characteristic we associate with sporting greats. Here was a boy who had ambition and refused to allow the reality of his life to deflect him away from that goal. Training to be a pilot is an expensive business and would not usually be the sort of job a poor child from the heart of Brazil could expect to achieve.

Because Pele was poor. Extremely so. It was rare that he could afford to buy himself a soccer ball. Instead, old socks filled with paper were the objects upon which he mastered his skills. Imagine a young child with talent today attempting to find their way into the professional game from that background. As soon as they are spotted, they can expect to be whisked away to the best academies, under the tutelage of the best coaches and with access to the best facilities, the best physical and emotional support and the best diet. For Pele, life was on the up when he could put away the paper stuffed sock and replace it with a mango to kick around.

For Pele, though, there were other factors which helped him to make it to the top. Of course, he was blessed with exceptional, phenomenal talents. Both those he could learn and perfect, such as passing and dribbling, but he was also endowed with less definable attributes. Even from young, he could read a game in a way that enabled him to be in the right place before his opponents. He could see a pass, and how a game would develop around him. It is true that experience develops a talent such as this, but some players – even very good ones – never really acquire it.

But on top of this he was also extremely quick, balanced and agile. A true athlete. In all probability, had the means and interest been there, he could have made it as a top performer in many sports. Yet soccer was in the boy's blood. Literally. Because his father Dodinho had been a professional footballer in has day as well, and he was prepared to ensure his son had every opportunity to make it to the top, something he had not quite managed to achieve himself.

There was another piece of good fortune which fell Pele's way. Timing. He grew up at a time when indoor football was growing in popularity in Brazil. For a player who would make his name for his touch and skill, this was perfect. Certainly, Brazilian soccer was already known for its extravagance and style, but the rough pitches used by the street players of the poor cities of Brazil could never allow skills such as those Pele held to develop.

The sacrifice of parents in the early years of their children's sporting careers are much reported. Maybe, though, for Dondinho, it was a little different. Even though he had played professionally, there was no money in the game in Brazil. At least, not for the players. In fact, he eventually gave up his career – he was a striker and played for a number of lower league teams – because he could not make ends meet. Dondinho now worked as a cleaner in a hospital, and although still extremely poor, at least the family had a more regular income.

However huge the ambitions of parents for their children, even he could not have imagined that Pele would turn into the player he became. Therefore, he knew that he was training his son up for a career which would deliver, he thought, at best a barely living wage. Yet he saw his son's passion, determination and willingness to learn. And he encouraged it; he taught Pele the tricks of his trade and saw in the boy a passion to improve.

Most of all, the two loved being in each other's company. This was no bullying relationship between over ambitious father seeking to live his own glory through his child. There was none of the Richard Williams' within him. Another three factors in the journey to the top – a huge appetite to learn allied to a coach with the expertise, the knowledge and the relationship to satisfy that appetite. All bound together with a love and joy that made learning not work, but pleasure.

Yet Pele was also brought down to earth by the person perhaps most important in his early life. His mother. 'My mother is a fantastic woman,' he once said. 'She always cared about my family, and my education. She taught me how to respect people. She gave me the opportunity to learn how to respect people.'

Celeste was also the realist in the family. She understood that life as a professional footballer was hard, and material rewards were few. 'In those early years,' recalled the great man, 'when she caught me playing soccer, she would give me a good verbal lashing. And sometimes much worse!'

Naturally enough, this determined and moral lady could not have guessed quite the achievements her son would make, nor how the world would change when it came to rewarding its sports players.

But we can draw many answers to the question of what makes a sporting great from the early life of Pele. Firstly, and without doubt, there must be the natural talent to stand out from the crowd. But that is only the starting point. Every sports fan could relate a dozen names of highly talented youngsters who never quite achieve their potential. For every one of those, there are dozens of others blessed with similar skills who never even make it to the public arena.

Pele demonstrates that a certain mindset is needed. There needs to be fire, determination, passion and even anger. A desire for victory. But that must be tempered by resilience. An ability to regard setbacks as a vital stepping stone on the path to success. The ability to see defeat in perspective, as something that happens and thus provides a lesson. Then is gone.

He also illustrates the importance of a love of his sport. How many hours must he have spent with his father, perfecting those skills which would soon light up the world? How could he have done that without loving what he was doing?

Pele also had a stable and loving upbringing – it was no doubt this that contributed to his mental and emotional strength. But, as the bullying he experienced and his poverty demonstrate, his secure home did not mean that life was not hard at times. That he overcame those challenges no doubt contributed to his resilience when it became apparent that the only way to stop Brazil was to stop him. By whatever means possible.

Then there was luck – particularly the genetic good fortune of having a father who was himself a fine player.

So, a complicated recipe, but maybe every single ingredient is required to turn a very good player into the greatest of all time. We shall see.

The Qualities That Made Pele Great

We will finish each chapter with a short recap on the attributes that turned the player into a great of the game. Since this book is one about the mindset of the best, we shall concentrate on that, and other factors outside of the physical ones the player possessed. Doing so should not detract from the fact that, above all, a player needs excellent athleticism, skill and technique to make it to the top. That point applies to every player in our list…in fact to every player who plays at the highest level. That we do not state this in every chapter does not reduce its significance…

For Pele:

- Huge strength of character to overcome bullying as a child.
- Poverty to inspire determination to lift himself out of it.
- A mentor – his father – able to teach him the game.
- Calmness of personality.
- A determination never to accept defeat.
- A love of the game, and the willingness to practise that love supported.
- A touch of fire.

- The good fortune of events coming together to encourage him to play the game.
- Loving parents, including a mother who kept the boy grounded.
- Loyalty allied to ambition.

28

The Player Who Could Not Avoid Politics

If Pele was the epitome of grace and style, our second all-time great fits another category entirely. **Ferenc Puskas** was the centerpiece of the **Magical Magyars** who were the most powerful international team on the planet in the decade following the second world war.

In 1953, England held an unbeaten record when playing at home. Eighty years without defeat. (To be fair, the degree of arrogance held by the English Football Association at the time - which still pervades to this day - slightly distorts this figure. The FA was careful to pick and choose its opponents. Up until 1950, the 'blazers' – as they are known - still regarded games against Scotland, Wales and Northern Ireland as the epitome of competition and until the Brazil tournament of that year refused to enter the World Cup.)

Nevertheless, Wembley truly was their castle. Then the Magyars arrived, and breached the walls. 6-3 the Hungarians won, and at the heart of the team was a slightly chubby, barrel chested individual. A man who used only his left foot, refused (most probably because of his lack of height) to engage in the aerial tennis that typified the British game in those days and who left opponents, including the great Billy Wright, tackling air and flat on their backside.

Another great, Sir Tom Finney, summed it all up. 'I came away wondering to myself what we had been doing all these years,' he said.

But if the stocky striker did not hold the classic build of a soccer player, there are a number of factors from his early life which mirror the experiences of the great Pele. Like the Brazilian, Ferenc Puskas (or Purczeld as he was known until the age of 10) entered the world straight into poverty. He was born in the capital, Budapest, although in one of its nicer parts, Zuglo. However, the family moved shortly after his birth. Their new home in Kispest was tiny – just two rooms which, perhaps fortuitously or perhaps significantly, overlooked the local football stadium, and indeed opened virtually onto the pitch. As for Kispest itself, it was a nice enough place in which to grow up. Located a few miles outside the center of Budapest, although it was a suburb of the capital it felt much more like a small town in its own right. It was modest but safe, and made a fair enough place for a small, football mad boy to pursue his passion.

Although he would become a stocky adult, Ferenc was slight as a boy. He played, barefooted (neither he nor his mates could afford boots) every moment that he could. There was no pitch as such, and the rough ground was littered with thistles and, sometimes, worse. A boy needed dedication to find fun playing on that. There was no ball, either, in those early days. Tightly packed wads of old rags were used as a substitute. It was only, as the young footballers could see their teens approaching over the horizon, that a youth team trainer saw them juggling and heading the pile of rags and invited them to use some of the Kispest club's old boots and balls. Soon, they had impressed enough to train with the proper youth players.

Like others among our list of greats, Puskas' father was also a useful player, who performed in the Hungarian leagues at a semi-professional level. Ferenc Purczeld Sr was a center half for the local Kispest team and went on to coach at the club after his retirement as a player. Not only did he help train his son but managed to 'confuse' his boy's age so that he, along with his close friend and neighbor, Jozsef Bozsik, could train at the club.

As with Pele, there were sometimes conflicts within the Puskas family; these lay between the young Ferenc and his mother. While the boy put football first, his mother concerned herself about injuries he got from playing on the thorn ridden fields, especially before he joined Kispest as a youth. She was worried about his commitment to soccer

31

above school. She was angered by his muddy clothing and torn shirts. They did not have much, the Puskas family, and the boy's mother could not bear to see what little they did own being ruined in chasing a ball substitute around a tussocky field. It was Puskas senior who intervened and kept the peace on these occasions. Reflections again of Pele's upbringing.

Ferenc was driven to improve. When his first proper coach, whom he called Uncle Nandi, told him he was too slow, he ran to school and raced tramcars to increase his speed. When the newly formed **Kispest** boys' team were losing their opening match, he set an example by taking off his uncomfortable boots and playing barefoot. His teammates did the same. He crawled under fences to get into the Kispest stadium to watch games. But despite his devotion, in his first autobiography Ferenc Puskas recalled the fun of playing. Of sweets at half time, and the joy of running and scoring. He experienced such a buzz from scoring that he was prepared to commit hours in his garden to perfecting skills and tricks. He idolized the professionals at Kispest, and also as a boy adored the English club Arsenal, who were the dominant force in English football as Ferenc was growing up in the early 1930s. It seems as though, even back then, soccer held an appeal across nations.

Around the outset of World War II, Ferenc senior was appointed manager of Kispest AC, and it was he who gave his son his first taste of league football, the boy making his debut at the age of 16 in 1943. But the story is not quite as straight forward as that, because by then Kispest were playing in the top league of Hungarian football. Yet they were still considered minnows of the game. But as the war ended, the communist Hungarian government took control of the club, renamed it **Honved** (which broadly translates to 'homeland defense') and focused on increasing recruitment of players from the army. Now able to pick from the most promising young talent around, the club grew in power – Honved's only rivals being MTK. They too had a recruitment advantage, drawing their players from the secret police, no less. Yet Honved were the top side and made up almost the entire national team. That, in part, explained the national team's (also known as Magical Magyars) enormous ability to play as a unit. Rather than being brought together a few times a year, as most international teams managed, they were playing together week in, week out, albeit under the banner of the Honved name.

By the time they arrived at Wembley in 1953 they had been unbeaten for three years and had lifted gold at the Helsinki Olympics of 1952. While gold at the Olympics hardly compares with winning the World Cup, nevertheless it was the point at which the strength of the

Magyars achieved wider recognition. 'It was during the Olympics that our football first started to flow with real power,' observed Puskas later.

Mind you, that tournament was dominated by the politics of Eastern Europe. In the first round, for example, Russia played Yugoslavia. 5-1 ahead with just half an hour to go, Yugoslavia managed to 'concede' four goals. However, they won the replay 3-1 and news of the defeat was kept quiet in the newly formed Soviet Union for over a year, in fact until after the death of Stalin. Russia had been expected to win the tournament, and defeat in the first round was not something to publicize under that regime.

Then came the Hungarian uprising. Honved were touring South America as the might of the Russian bear snuffed out a Hungarian revolution. It was a trigger, and Puskas decided to defect rather than return to his homeland. He was not alone, others who made the decision to take their talents elsewhere included the prolific forward Sandor Kocsis and Puskas' long time childhood friend, Josef Bozsik.

It must have been a terribly difficult decision and is perhaps evidence of the mental strength Ferenc Puskas possessed to not only put his career on hold (he was banned from world football for eighteen months by the Hungarian FA) but also to leave his family and friends behind. It would be close to forty years before he could return to his homeland. Of course, in the end the Galloping Major joined Real Madrid, forming a lasting and enduring partnership with Alberto Di Stefano, although apparently the two did not get on terribly well as people. Perhaps another sign of the self-belief and determination needed to be a top striker. Maybe the selfishness as well.

The signing was controversial. Other members of the Honved side who defected joined rivals Barcelona, but when Puskas joined Real, there were real concerns about his age – he was 31, getting old for the day – and his fitness. The doubters should not have worried.

Unlike Pele, Ferenc Puskas never lifted the World Cup, although he did secure an Olympic medal. Hungary was the best team at the 1954 World Cup tournament held in Switzerland by a country mile but lost in the final to West Germany 3-2. In fact, they had already thrashed the Germans during the group stage, beating them 8-3. (It was a tournament with a remarkable number of goals scored, 140 in 26 matches. The Magyars contributed twenty-seven of these in their five matches.) By the '58 finals, politics had superseded sport, Hungary had been subsumed into the Soviet Union and the team had broken up. But even if he never quite saw the **Magical Magyars** fulfil their potential on the world stage, Puskas achieved astonishing levels of success at club level.

Playing with the Army team, **Honved**, in Hungary, Puskas won five domestic championships, scoring an astonishing 357 goals in just 354 games in the process. One nickname which attached to him was the 'Galloping Major', itself a reference to the fact that Honved was the Hungarian Army team. He also achieved an equally impressive scoring rate with the Magyars, 83 in 84 internationals. However, it is probably with Real Madrid that he gained his greatest fame. (Although, who can guess how many times he would have played and scored with his national team without the intervention of communism? He was in his prime when the team broke up.)

Puskas' record with the Spanish giants, Real Madrid, is truly remarkable. 512 goals in 528 appearances. Five Spanish league titles, three Spanish Cups, an Intercontinental Cup and, best of all, three European Cups (as well as a hat-trick in one of the finals they actually lost.)

In fact, Ferenc Puskas had almost become a Manchester United player prior to joining the Spanish giants. Following the tragedy of the Munich air crash, United were desperately seeking to find players to join their team. For a while, it seemed as though one would be the Hungarian. However, the deal fell through, and it is not completely clear why. One reason could have been the wage cap in England at the time – the £20 per week maximum United would have been permitted to pay was thirty times less than Puskas could earn at Real. There was also concern about the philosophy of the club – that players should be English. (Remember, the Empire was still lingering on in those days, and 'foreigners' were somehow distrusted). Most probably, in the end, it was the intransigence of the English FA which stopped one of the greatest players of all time from appearing on British soil.

Who knows, had Puskas been allowed to join United, his true genius might have been recognized even more, and his deserved place up there in the echelons of the best two or three players of all time secured.

He died in November 2006 at the age of 79, having succumbed to the long and difficult journey of Alzheimer's at the turn of the millennium. If it were needed, and it is not, his legacy could be ensured through the Puskas award which is given each season to the goal judged the best in Europe.

One huge fan is Sir Alex Ferguson, former Manchester United manager. The tough Scot saw Puskas score four against Eintracht Frankfurt in the 1960 European Cup final which took place in Glasgow's Hampden Park.

'I was at the European Cup final in 1960,' he said, 'but I also saw him score the only goal against Rangers at Ibrox, before he got a hat-trick against them when Real scored six in the second leg. In his day he was a special player without question, part of that great period for Hungarian football. How they did not win the World Cup in 1954 is beyond me.'

Beyond most others, as well.

The Qualities That Made Puskas Great

- The passion which can be driven by the wish to escape from poverty.
- A small build which made him develop perfect technique.
- Mentors in his father, a player himself, and the coach of his local youth team.
- A love for the sport, which meant he was prepared to play using rags as a ball and on the most uncomfortable playing surfaces.
- The motivation of living on the doorstep of the Kispest stadium.
- Mental strength to be a winner, and the strength to make tough decisions, such as leaving his homeland behind.

- The fortune to be around as his local club were reviewing their youth policy, making it more inclusive.

The Purveyor of Total Football

Onto another player now who also almost achieved the highest glory on the international stage. The Dutch master, **Johan Cruyff**. If Ferenc Puskas' legacy continues through the Puskas Award for the best goal in a given season, then Cruyff has his own piece of footballing magic to carry his name. The Cruyff turn. The forward first made the world gasp with this piece of skill on the biggest platform, the World Cup of 1974. Sweden were the poor team mesmerized by this mastery.

For any who have yet to see this mind-blowing piece of skill in action, get onto YouTube quickly, and find the clips. Cruyff faces one way, moves his marker in that direction, hooks the ball with his instep, changes direction 180 degrees and with a knock is away, the defender left marking empty air. But if Cruyff and Puskas are remembered through a particular aspect of their play, physically they are marked by their different physiques.

While Puskas was the barrel-chested, stocky little guy, low center of balance enabling him to twist defenders this way and that; Cruyff was tall, slim as a pole, languid – a man who played the game with all the time in the world. It appears as though Johan Cruyff never breaks sweat, never exerts himself. Yet he dominates the pitch.

In Cruyff's birth and early childhood (note: his surname is actually spelt Cruijff) we see a remarkable similarity to that of Ferenc Puskas. While young Hendrik Johannes Cruijff might not be able to open a window of his house and look out on a football stadium, he still lived just a minute's walk from the home of mighty Ajax. It is hard not to draw conclusions about their childhood spent so close to an iconic soccer ground. That somehow living in such proximity to the stadium each would later make their first professional soccer home had an influence on these two as boys. The atmosphere, the magic, the ethereal presence of the pitch, especially on match days, must surely have played its part in driving not only Puskas but Cruyff too into the professional game.

Another factor which is emerging consistently from their childhoods is that our soccer greats came from humble backgrounds. This is certainly true for Johan Cruyff. He may have looked like an aristocrat on the pitch, but nothing could be further than the truth in his upbringing. Yet like Puskas and Pele, and indeed many more of the greats we will consider, Cruyff was motivated by his father's love of the game. A reasonable amateur player himself, Hermanus Cruyff dedicated his life to his second son, teaching him skills and encouraging him to develop his attributes.

The youth set up at Ajax is rightly regarded for its excellence. Young Johan was fortunate to join its ranks at a time of particular innovation at the club. He was just ten years old at the time. But tragedy struck the family two years later when Hermanus died from a heart attack. It is a sign of the emotional strength of the child that he not only coped with the loss of his father but used his death to motivate himself further towards becoming a professional player.

Johan Cruyff broke into the Ajax starting lineup as an eighteen-year-old, and scored twenty-five goals in his debut season, helping the side to win the Dutch first division. His emergence coincided with the arrival of the coach who would transform Ajax from an average Dutch first division team to European champions. Rinus Michels. The architect of the total football tactics which revolutionized the game. An achievement he could not have made without his star man. 'Without Cruyff,' he said, 'I have no team.' A slight exaggeration of fact, but his meaning is clear enough.

Although the player was nominally a center forward, this was the era of Total Football. As such, every player was required to perform in any position. It was a role that the mercurial striker fitted into easily, and he was as adept at dropping into midfield, or moving onto the wing, as he was at bursting through the middle of the pitch and bearing down on goal.

In fact, Ajax went on to win the Eredivisie in the next two seasons as well, three in a row during a run of six titles in eight seasons, and with Cruyff as their talismanic striker, also reached the final of the European Cup, although they were beaten by AC Milan. However, total football was beginning to dominate not only in the Netherlands, but across the whole of Europe. By the 1970-71 season, Ajax were ready to claim the trophy that their soccer deserved and won the title by beating the Greek side Panathinaikos 2-0 in the final at Wembley. This was the first of three consecutive European titles for the team, Cruyff to the fore. The striker scored both goals in the 1972 victory over Inter Milan.

As well as team triumphs, Cruyff received personal recognition during this spell. He won the Ballon d'Or on three occasions, in 1971, 1973 and 1974, although by the latter two of these he had moved across Europe to join Barcelona, following Michels to the Spanish giants. His departure marked the end of Ajax's European dominance. 1974 was also the year of Cruyff's World Cup. His Dutch team, with their own Ajax inspired brand of total football, dominated the tournament. They reached the final conceding just a single goal and led that match after just two minutes. Cruyff himself was named 'Best Player' of the tournament. West Germany, though, hit back to secure the trophy 2-1.

It was to be the maestro's first and last World Cup. By the time of the 1978 finals, concerns over his personal safety, and that of his family, persuaded Cruyff to withdraw from selection for the Dutch squad. Internal troubles in Spain had led to him being targeted by kidnap threats. As important as soccer might be, Cruyff placed the safety of his family and himself first. The Dutch reached the final once more and may well have won the tournament had their best player been available.

Cruyff went on to become a fine manager in his own right and is widely credited for laying down the structures and philosophy that underpinned the hugely successful playing style for which Barcelona become noted in the 2000s and 2010s. He has been described by the respected soccer journalist and writer, Graham Hunter, as the 'single most important man in the history of organized football.' In terms of soccer alone, it is hard to argue with that. (Later, we will consider Maradona's influence on the lives of a nation, beyond the world of soccer. Cruyff, though, is surely the most influential figure from within the game.)

He possessed the balance of a ballerina, the intelligence of a scientist, the agility of a gymnast, the vision of an artist and the athleticism of, well, a professional soccer player at the top of his game. Unlike many others who achieved iconic status as players, he was also a genius as a manager and coach. Too often, the greatest players cannot make this transition. Their skills and technique come too naturally to them, and they find it hard to explain how their players can improve. The best coaches have the authority of a leader and the communication talents of the finest teachers.

Cruyff possessed all of these attributes, but even more still. He was on top of everything he personally brought to soccer, and to Barcelona in particular, and was able to lay down an influence that lasted well beyond his days in the dugout. Consider Barcelona's greatest three players of its time as the world leader of club soccer. Would Iniesta have made it to the top without Cruyff's influence? Probably not. The young, small kid who made his debut would have been classed as too young and too small by most coaches. The same could be said for Xavi. And, without Cruyff's influence, the best of them all, Lionel Messi, would have been sent back to Argentina before his brilliance could offer a glare more dazzling than the brightest floodlights.

But if Johann Cruyff was a man who could lay down a genuine, long lasting legacy, he was also a man of his time. It seems strange to imagine the case today, but off the pitch Cruyff would often be photographed with a cigarette in his mouth. He was a heavy smoker. Following double heart surgery in 1991, he gave up tobacco, famously swapping the killer for lollipops. He participated in a health campaign, uttering the words: 'Football has given me everything in life, tobacco almost took it all away.' The 'almost' proved premature, in 2015 he issued an announcement stating that he was suffering from lung cancer but offering the cheering news that he was defeating the disease. The upbeat message was wrong, and he died in 2016. He was just 68 years old.

As would be expected, tributes to his mastery of the sport came in from across the world. The Dutch FA perhaps summed feelings up: 'Words can hardly be found for this huge loss,' it said, before going on to describe its son as the 'greatest Dutch footballer of all time, and one of the world's best ever.'

Yet Cruyff's record as a player and manager is without equal. On top of his 293 goals in 521 top class appearances for his five clubs, (204 of these for Ajax) he won the following: 13 domestic cup competitions, 14 domestic league titles, 4 European Cups and 7 other European titles.

As great as this record is, it falls behind the great man's legacy. Soccer is the beautiful game, but sometimes it has become inured in negativity, in the dominance of defense. Cruyff took the sport and made it wonderful to watch.

It is probably true to say that, as superb as he was, he would not sit at the top of this list of greatest players. But in terms of his overall influence on the game, Cruyff is the master among masters. Not bad for a man from such humble beginnings.

The Qualities That Made Cruyff Great

- Overcoming the challenges of growing up in relative poverty.
- The lure of the Ajax Stadium close to his home.
- The influence of his father and mentor, himself a good soccer player.
- The commitment of his parents to giving the young Cruyff the opportunity to succeed.
- The strength of character to overcome the sudden death of his father when Cruyff was still a child, and to use that grief to drive him towards greatness.
- The fortune to burst into the game at a time a visionary coach arrived to take Ajax to unprecedented levels of success.

- Intelligence and the talent to be one of the sport's global leaders.

The Two Modern Masters

A brief look at the list of Ballon d'Or winners explains why these two are given a chapter to share. We can start in 2007, when the award was presented to the Brazilian, Kaka. A fine player, without question, but it is the two young stars who sat close together beneath him that year who are significant. A young Manchester United winger, **Cristiano Ronaldo**. Followed narrowly by a Barcelona player on the threshold of greatness, **Lionel Messi**.

We shift forward to the 2019 winner, the last to be named at the time of writing since in 2020 Covid intervened, and the award was not presented. Over those twelve years between Kaka and the present time, on just one occasion has somebody other than Ronaldo or Messi been declared the world's best player. That was in 2018, when Luka Modric was named winner. Messi has achieved the title six times, his Portuguese peer five. Almost as incredible, during nine of those twelve years, the couple have shared the top two positions in the vote.

Such rivalry leads to the inevitable question of who the better player is. The answer to that one lies in the eye of the beholder. Both are strikers, each are phenomenal goal scorers. They are, though, very different players.

Ronaldo is a winger turned central striker, Messi a deeper lying forward. Both have astonishing close control, explosive pace and the ability to produce in the biggest of matches. Ronaldo is the better in the air, a player possessing the talent to hang suspended above ground before tensing those enormous neck muscles and powering the ball goalward. Messi is perhaps the stronger team player, more willing to bring teammates into the game and create chances for them. Certainly, this is true since Ronaldo switched to a more central role in around 2010.

Maybe being named after Ronald Reagan is not the most auspicious start in life. Although, that was the fate which faced the young Ronaldo. Strangely the boy was given the name, so the story goes, less for support of the right-wing president's politics than his dubious skills as a film actor. The man best remembered (artistically) for acting beside a chimpanzee seems an unlikely hero. The superstar-to-be was born in 1985 and grew up overlooking the ocean from his Portugal home. If that sounds idyllic; it wasn't. Ronaldo's first residence being somewhat different to the mansions he enjoys today. This one was a tin-roofed shanty, a working-class lean-to shack,

50

furthering the evidence that many of the greatest soccer players began their lives in the humblest of homes. As with the other players we have seen so far, Ronaldo's father was a great influence on his earliest years in the game. Unlike some of the others, however, Cristiano's father – Dinis Aveiro – was a keen follower of soccer rather than an expert participant. He did still hold an interest in the game beyond that of being a fan and spectator. He acted as kit man for a local youth team, and it was through this contact that Ronaldo began his formal soccer career at the age of eight. In fact, Dinis was a gardener who worked for the local municipality, and Ronaldo's mother, Maria Dolores dod Santos Aveiro, like others seeking to get what they could from a meagre existence, worked many jobs, including as a cook and cleaner.

The boy put his soccer over his schoolwork and would climb out of his bedroom window to play the game rather than spend hours ensconced in the hot room completing his homework. Indeed, schooling seemed like a chore for the talented sportsman. Apparently, he once threw a chair at a teacher who, in his opinion, had insulted him. This passion shows itself on the pitch. He is a natural leader and a senior player, as he was a dominant personality as a child. Indeed, just as in his heyday, the young Ronaldo was renowned for his speed and athleticism as much as his footballing skills.

Indeed, that self-belief which told him he was justified in reacting angrily to his teacher is another characteristic that the young Ronaldo took into his adulthood. Sometimes, his manner is described as arrogant; in truth it is not. Simply, he believes he is the best, and that motivates him to do what it takes to be recognized as the best. Then, he possessed the self-belief to hold onto that accolade as he moved through the ranks of the game. In that respect, nothing has changed. Even approaching his late thirties, he still takes all of Portugal's penalties and free kicks in shooting range. He is still the main man. No question.

Young Ronaldo progressed quickly. By the age of ten he was on the books of a well-regarded local club, Nacional, winning the U13 Regional Championships with the club. This was in 1995-96, meaning the boy was just aged ten or eleven throughout that campaign, two or three years younger than most of his rivals – and team mates. It is not surprising that he soon came to the attention of Sporting CP, one of Portugal's leading club sides. Yet despite his phenomenal early progress, once more good fortune would play a significant part in the playing life of a great. He was only fifteen when a rare medical condition which caused his heart to race uncontrollably and unpredictably was spotted. It could have spelled the end of a burgeoning future, but Sporting was ahead of the game and had the resources to send their young starlet for an operation which repaired the condition. Soon he was playing once more, achieving the remarkable feat of progressing through the Under 16, 17, 18 and B Sporting teams in the space of a season, before making his debut for the first team.

Arsenal, Liverpool and Barcelona were among Europe's great teams who courted the dazzling winger, but it was Alex Ferguson, at Manchester United, who secured his services. It was shortly after joining the Manchester club that the sort of personal tragedy which seems too regular an occurrence in the lives of greats hit Ronaldo. Despite the incredibly close relationship he held with his father, and despite the excellent support he provided as his son's mentor, Dinis suffered from alcohol addiction. Cristiano was just twenty when his father died from kidney failure, and he was left to rue the reluctance of his father to accept his own advice for once, and to go into rehab to break the cycle of alcoholism that was cutting short his life.

To return to Ferguson, there can be little doubt that the great man-manager played a major part in delivering the player Cristiano Ronaldo became. As a youngster, on the wing, Ronaldo could be inconsistent. His decision making could be awry, and that self-belief could sometimes translate itself into selfishness in the soccer sense. Ferguson stuck by his youth, encouraging him, and improving him. A lesser coach may have tried to rein in his wilder soccer playing excesses, rather than let them develop, and trust in the player's own determination to reach the very top of the game. It takes little more than a glance at Ronaldo's trophy cabinet to realize that he does truly deserve his place among the other champions in this book.

On top of his Ballon d'Or awards, which he won (in its various forms) in 2008, 2013, 2014, 2016 and 2017, and numerous footballer of the year awards, and sportsman of the year titles, it is in the acquisition of major team trophies that his record becomes even more remarkable. The English FA Cup in 2004 and runners-up in two of the next three years, runners up in the European Championships of 2004, third in 2012 and winners in 2016. Two League Cups in 2006 and 2009, Premierships in 2007, 2008 and 2009. La Liga titles in 2012 and 2017 before bagging the Serie A with Juventus in his first two seasons there. The Copa Del Ray in 2011 and 2014 and the Coppa Italia in 2020-21. Numerous Super Cups of various denominations also grace whichever room of whichever house Ronaldo keeps his trophies. But pride of place must go to that gold medal from the 2016 European Championships, the winners' medal from the inaugural UEFA Nations League and, of course, the Champions League titles he helped to secure for Manchester United in the 2007-8 season, and for Real Madrid in 2014, 2016, 2017 and 2018.

At the time of writing this book, the European Championships are playing out across Europe. Cristiano Ronaldo is 36 years old. At the end of the group stages, he has scored five goals in three games for Portugal. At those 36 years of age, he leads the scoring charts by two goals after just those three games. In Portugal's group were Hungary, a middling team, but also the might of tournament favorites France, and perennial achievers Germany. So not only has he scored twice in two matches, and once in the other one, but he has achieved this feat against very strong opposition. And, he has achieved this in a Portugal team which has struggled in all of its games. (In fact, they went out in the last 16, beaten by the number one ranked team in the world, Belgium.) Time must surely defeat him one day, but at the moment it seems as though Ronaldo really will go on forever.

That sense is not just down to hyperbole; Cristiano Ronaldo is an athlete of phenomenal proportions. Of our ten greats, he is possibly, in athletic terms alone, the finest of the group. That commitment to supreme fitness and strength is delivering continued rewards in terms of the longevity of his career.

Three themes which might epitomize the mindset of the greatest soccer players are beginning to emerge. The first is background. Sitting somewhere on the line between uncomfortable poverty and absolute impoverishment is a common thread among the players we have looked at so far. It is worth spending a while considering this factor. Does the desire to escape from a poor background drive a player on, inculcating them with a never say die attitude which transfers itself from the streets to the world's biggest stadia?

It is an easy conclusion to draw that soccer is a poor person's game. Yet that is not absolutely the case. Yes, the simplicity of the sport undoubtedly makes it accessible to those who have the least. One cannot become a great golfer without access to expensive courses and equipment (never mind coaching!) The same applies to tennis. Despite worthy attempts across the world to make the sport more accessible, the fact remains that in order to become a top player, years of coaching are required. And that means access to courts that are high quality. It is not impossible to become an international tennis player from a working-class background, but it is extremely difficult. In the UK, and many other countries, scholarship schemes exist whereby children are spotted at a relatively young age – typically 10 or 11 – and their parents are offered awards which usually include coaching at a very high standard. However, there are two significant downsides to this – under the British system at least. Firstly, in order to be able to access the sort of quality of coaching required to make it to the top (these scholarships seek to find future international players, not just club professionals) hubs are required to maximize the efficient use of coaches' time. Simple park courts are also of too low quality for such training, and specialized surfaces are needed. That means usually moving children away from their homes and families, and into independent boarding schools where such facilities exist.

Thus, youngsters face not only the hours of training they will require to make it to the top, but also being dragged away from their families and support networks into an alien environment just as they are reaching the challenging times of puberty and adolescence. It is not surprising that success is rare.

The second problem relates to the first. In order to be spotted as a ten-year-old, a lot of work needs already to have been done, which means the children who appear the best at that age are necessarily from wealthy backgrounds.

There are working class sports, of course. Boxing comes to mind, and also athletics often attracts participants from a wide background. But while soccer is undoubtedly a sport which attracts working class players, it is not just a working-class sport. Its origins are often listed as being from the industrial heartlands of Britain. Wealthy factory owners setting up teams to offer entertainment and exercise to their workers, who frequently lived in factory owned houses in the vicinity of their work. There is truth in that. Take a trip to some of the older grounds in the UK and usually they will be situated among the terraced houses of the Victorian and Edwardian eras.

Some of those factory owners were self-made men, but most already had money. And that meant they themselves had been educated at public schools – the Harrows, Winchesters and Marlborough of the British system. It was in institutions that these men learned of football – albeit in highly localized forms. That was the game they took to their workers, and which was then quickly formalized into the forerunner of the game we knew today.

It might be a surprise that a child who gains a place at Eton College, probably the most elite school on the entire planet, will put on a soccer strip when they go for their numerous sports lessons. Other sports thrive at the school situated on the Berkshire Thames – rugby, tennis, golf, Eton Fives and even the oddly structured Eton Wall Game (a sort of rugby and soccer mix) but soccer is the main sport at this hotbed of privilege.

So, yes working-class people play football, but it is not their exclusive reserve.

In addition to the significance of a working-class background the role of a mentor – often the player's father – appears to have played a major part in creating the best players. The third theme to begin to emerge is that the very best players seem to each have overcome a major adversity in their lives, particularly when they are still children, or very young adults.

This third factor was eminently present in the life of Ronaldo's great rival, Luis Lionel Andres Messi. A couple of years younger than Ronaldo, Messi belongs among that group of top players for whom a very short stature gives them balance and agility, turning them into phenomenal dribblers of the ball. Puskas was another in this category, and later we will consider perhaps the finest dribbler of them all, Diego Maradona. Messi is 5 feet 7 inches tall. For much of his youth it seemed that attaining such a height would be a forlorn dream.

There could be no doubting the young Leo's talents. Or his courage. The tiny boy entered fearlessly into games with his older brothers and their mates, easily standing his ground and coming back for more when he was driven off the ball by the bigger, stronger and older boys. But he did not grow. Yet his talents even as an eight-year-old were quickly recognized. This was the age at which he was taken on by Newell's Old Boys, a strong local club based in his home city of Rosario, one which had a strong youth system.

It was hard to say back then whether Messi was more recognizable for the height gap between himself and his team mates, or for his stunning talents with the ball. To begin with, it was probably the latter, but as his peers grew, and began to accelerate in height and build as puberty knocked on their doors, little Lionel remained resolutely small. The gap grew and the family dream that Lionel could make the grade as a soccer player began to fade.

Skill, technique, pace and bravery make up for a lot, but if a child simply cannot achieve all their potential dictates because of their physical build, they will begin to fall behind. Lionel's parents were Jorge and Celia, and they were typical of the working class parents we have seen already in this book. Totally committed to their child's interests and needs, as supportive as they could be but very poor. Still, they took their boy to seek medical means to address his small stature. His doctors were clear – the only way Lionel would grow would be to follow a long course of injections. His small size was the result of a hormone deficiency which led to restricted growth. Without the treatment, there was no chance that he would have any kind of future in the sport he loved, and more than that, he would always remain notably small.

There was no question. Their son must have the treatment. But there was a downside. The injections were expensive and would cost several hundred dollars per month. Money the family did not have. Nevertheless, they began the course, working overtime to raise the money they needed. For a while, they managed through their commitment and the support of friends and family. But it could not last, and it seemed as though the world would be denied the sight of Lionel Messi in full flow spotlighted in one of the world's great stadiums.

Soccer clubs are often accused of lacking foresight; of being results driven institutions who give little thought to the future. The academy programs around the world give lie to that easy conclusion, even though is probably contains an element of truth. Certainly, Barcelona deserve credit for taking the considerable gamble of supporting a small child with heaven in his boots and seeing in him the potential to be one of the best of all time, and probably the best of his particular era. Lionel Messi is, at the time of writing, a one club man. Even though he seems to be expressing some dissatisfaction with the current, 2021 set up, he has repaid Barcelona's support many times over by giving them his very best years. But well done to the Catalan team for spotting potential over stature.

The club agreed to take on the boy, and ensure he received whatever medication was necessary to help him grow physically and become big and strong enough to compete at the highest level. Lionel was 13 at the time, and the condition for receiving this treatment was one he could not take on alone. Because Barcelona was prepared to take the gamble, a team from Spain and not Argentina. And so, the decision was made; the entire family upped sticks and headed across the equator and over the Atlantic, there to settle in the beautiful city that was home to the Spanish giants.

To make such a move demonstrated an astonishing level of commitment not only from Jorge and Celia, but from Lionel's siblings as well. While perhaps his parents were prepared to give up jobs as a steelworker and cleaner respectively, for Rodrigo and Matias, along with sister Maria Sol, the change must have been challenging. But they made it, and we see once more a great of the game coming from a family who offered total, unconditional support.

While many of us were unfortunate enough not to see Pele play, or Puskas or even Cruyff in his prime the same is unlikely to be true for

Messi and Ronaldo. Fortunate fans will have seen them in the flesh, and surely all of us have witnessed their astonishing exploits on TV or via the internet. So, there is little need to highlight the brilliance of Lionel Messi, a man who in a moment of sheer magnificence can win a game for Barcelona or, less often it has to be admitted, Argentina. Maybe that is another point of separation of the two greats of the current game. While Ronaldo has been the icing on the cake in a period of Portuguese strength at international level, Messi has had the lesser fortune of representing Argentina during one of the more fallow patches in its international soccer history.

One Under 20 World Cup winners medal, runners up in the main competition in 2014, three runners up medals in the Copa America. For most players, it would be a haul of which to be proud. Maybe for Messi that is less so. Especially when compared to his trophies and awards earned as a Barcelona player. Of course, for much of Messi's career the Catalans have been among the top three teams in Europe (and probably, therefore, the world) and often they have headed that triumvirate. No doubt that is partly due to having Messi in the team, and also partly due to the quality of player attracted by the thought of appearing in the same side as the maestro. There are his six Ballon d'Or awards, and countless trophies for golden boots, player of the season and such like. But consider his list of team competition victories. 4 Champions League titles, 10 Spanish championships, 3 Supercups, 7 Spanish cups, one more Spanish Supercup victory. An incredible collection of titles.

Still there is more to Messi than that. He truly lights up the field of play when he is out there. He is genuinely a genius, and one who can produce it time and time again in the very biggest of matches. The mental fortitude to do that is yet another trait of the greatest players.

Ronaldo too is a fine player to watch, and he was especially exciting with the ball at his feet in his younger days. His ability to bamboozle defenders with multiple stepovers was something magical to behold. As the Portuguese matured, and switched to a more central role, he became a devastating goal scorer.

But if Ronaldo sets the fans alive, Messi sets them alight. To see him dribbling through impossible spaces, demonstrating such close control, such balance, such vision and agility prior to unleashing an unerring shot or outstanding assist is to witness true inspiration, with all the thrill that brings.

There are many fans for whom Ronaldo is peerless. It is unquestionable that he and Messi are to date the two finest players of the 21st century. But, as controversial as this might seem, it is hard for the neutral not to conclude that of the pair, it is Messi who they would choose to watch both today and at the peak of their respective powers.

Although, of course, ideally, we would watch them both in action. Even, in the same game.

The Qualities That Make Ronaldo Great

- Overcoming considerable poverty.
- Parents who worked long hours to provide for him.
- A father who acted as mentor and introduced him to people who could further his potential. Later, a great mentor in Sir Alex Ferguson who both developed the young player, and kept his feet firmly anchored to the floor. (Apart from when he was skipping past full backs.)
- A dominant personality and leadership skills.
- A love of soccer above all else.
- Passion.
- The emotional strength to get over the loss of his father at an early age, and also to recover from his own career and life-threatening heart condition.
- Self-belief.
- An astonishing personal drive towards achieving and maintaining fitness and strength.

The Qualities That Make Messi Great

- A humble upbringing.

- Astonishing commitment to him by his parents and siblings, travelling across the world so he could receive the medical treatment needed for him to make it as a soccer player.
- Great commitment to him by his parents.
- A small stature which meant he needed to develop extreme skill and technique to thrive as a young child.
- The fortune to be spotted by a club with the means and foresight to see potential over physical stature.
- Loyalty.
- Bravery. Physical and emotional.
- Overcoming the disadvantage of always being the smallest as a child. The strength of character this helped to develop.

Bonus #2:

I hope you enjoyed the previous chapter on Messi vs Ronaldo. If you did, you'll love our next bonus. It's a 1-page printable infographic timeline on the careers of Messi and Ronaldo. Just scan the QR code below to access it.

A Short message from the Author:

Hey, are you enjoying the book? I'd love to hear your thoughts!

Many readers do not know how hard reviews are to come by, and how much they help an author.

I would be incredibly thankful if you could take just 60 seconds to write a brief review on Amazon, even if it's just a few sentences!

Your review will genuinely make a difference for me and help gain exposure for my work.

Outspoken and Outstanding

When a person, or an object, becomes a verb in the English language, it truly has arrived. The bosses at the electrical giants must feel a shiver of joy whenever they hear a consumer announce that they need to 'hoover the lounge'. So, it must bring a smile to the face of the great goalkeeper whenever Peter Schmeichel hears a fan or commentator announce that a goalkeeper has 'Schmeicheled it.' Even autocorrect on Word recognizes the term, so accepted has it become!

To Schmeichel – the verb means to close down the opponent in a one-on-one attack between striker and keeper. To stay upright for as long as possible, forcing the striker to make a decision, before throwing all four limbs in opposite directions at the moment of the forward's shot, presenting a larger target than seems naturally possible for a human being to make. Peter Schmeichel appeared to have an advantage in this field. It always looked as though he possessed eight limbs, rather than the requisite two arms and two legs.

In a one on one with the keeper, the expectation is usually that the striker will score. Given a bit of time and a good angle, they will find the net in about 70-80% of cases. Not with Schmeichel standing between them and celebration. When our team's center forward bore down on his goal, defenders trailing in his wake, fans knew that the job of scoring had only just begun. There was still well over half the task to complete. It was a pleasant surprise rather than an expectation when the ball ended up in the net. Schmeichel was that good.

During much of the keeper's career with Manchester United two teams dominated English football. The tough, pragmatic United created by Sir Alex Ferguson and the flowing, mercurial Arsenal of Arsene Wenger. When it came to the joy of watching them, most neutrals agreed that the London reds of Arsenal were the ones to pick, but when it came to winning trophies, the reds of Manchester held the edge. Most probably, the reason for that was Peter Schmeichel, such was his dominance in goal, and so considerable were his organizational skills with the Manchester United defense. Simply, that self-assurance which is the hallmark of the best strikers wavered in the face of the tall, well-built, blond Dane.

Peter Boleslaw Schmeichel was born to a Polish father and Danish mother on November 18th, 1963, in a suburb of Copenhagen. In fact, the great Dane could have played for Poland, holding Polish citizenship until 1970, when he and his siblings, along with his father, became Danish citizens. They say that goalkeepers are different, and this certainly seems to have been the case when we compare Schmeichel's formative years with those of his peers from this book. He grew up in Buddinge, a small village which was gradually subsumed into the growing spread of Copenhagen, joining the Gladsaxe municipality. Located close to lakes and the coast, Buddinge is far removed from the built-up tenements and shacks in which many of our other soccer players spent their early years.

Schmeichel's youth was financially more comfortable as well. His mother, Inger, was a nurse and his father a jazz musician. Theirs was a relatively comfortable, artistic upbringing in which Peter and his sisters thrived.

As for the keeper's trophy laden career, two moments stick out. Winning the treble in 1999 with Manchester United, and his astonishing feat of winning the Euros with Denmark in 1992. 'Those things are the highlights of my career and something that I will look back on with so much pleasure for the rest of my life. I'm one of the lucky guys,' he said. 'I played with some of the best players in the world and we achieved so many things.' For those too young to recall, the 1992 victory was all the more remarkable given that Denmark had not even qualified for the finals. However, they got a last-minute call up when Yugoslavia, in those days the country still existed, were banned following an escalation of the troubles in the Balkans. Soon, the region would become embroiled in that terrible war of the early 1990s.

With Denmark finishing behind Yugoslavia in their qualifying group, the Danes were promoted to the competition proper. It was fortunate that the squad was actually preparing for a friendly game at the time, and so were all together, although many players had the intention of heading to the beach once their season was completed. Nevertheless, Schmeichel recalls an end of term feeling among the camp, and the idea that they could become tournament ready in just a few days was unthinkable. There were presumably a lot of disappointed wives and girlfriends who suddenly saw their summer sun experience put on hold.

As for the Danish coach, Richard Moller Nielsen, he had organized for a new kitchen to be fitted while the Euros were on. Another change of plan required – let's hope he still managed to find a last-minute plumber. Although, he was probably prepared to put up with a delay to his domestic arrangements in return for a winners' medal at the competition. Not that the prospect of that entered his head.

With Schmeichel in goal, the Danish side earned a creditable 0-0 draw with a strong England team in their opener. England had recently reached the semi-finals of the World Cup and would go on to be semifinalists once more at the 1996 Euros. Schmeichel recalls a touch of disappointment with the result. Having felt just happy to be at the jamboree, the team were disappointed not to secure a major upset by beating the English. 'We all felt we should have won,' he recalled.

However, maybe it was the freedom bought by lack of pressure which saw that result surprisingly achieved, because as the Danes suddenly realized they were not just there to make up the numbers, their performance levels dropped. In the second match, which they lost 1-0 to neighbors and hosts, Sweden, they were well beaten. With unfortunate hyperbole, 'Denmark are out!' scolded a Danish TV commentator following that defeat. Maybe he had a point, because the loss left the Danes bottom of the group with one match to go. That was against an up-and-coming France team who were in fact the tournament favorites. Led by a former player whose presence could easily have been recorded in this book, Michel Platini, the French also boasted players of the caliber of Papin and Cantona in their side.

However, the French had so far been disappointing in the tournament despite entering the competition with a 100% record in qualifying. Draws against Sweden and England had left them needing to win to qualify. Given the slightly bloated nature of modern

74

competitions, it might be strange to recall that this European Championship featured just two groups of four teams (there were fewer independent countries in Europe in those days, as well), with the top two qualifying from each mini league. But with Denmark taking the lead twice against the fancied French, it was the two underdogs, Sweden and Denmark, who ended up qualifying from their group, with the French propping up the table.

The other group, however, delivered more expected outcomes. Here, the mighty Germans came second to the even more enterprising Netherlands team. Scotland were third, and the favorites of pub quizzes, the CIS, ended up bottom of that group. The CIS were, for those whose memory on the subject is a little shaky, a transitional team representing the former Soviet Union. That had ceased to exist at the end of 1991, but with the then Soviet team having already qualified, the CIS were a conglomeration of Russians and players from former members of the Soviet Union. The CIS was disbanded after the competition.

The Danes progressed to the final by beating the best team in the competition, the Netherlands, 5-4 on penalties. Then they comfortably out-did Germany 2-0 in the final itself. So, in only actually winning two out of five games in normal time (drawing two and losing one), the Danes had no easy path to lifting their only ever international trophy.

Maybe it was the lack of pressure in the build up to the tournament, when the only stress was whether the sun would shine on the players' summer breaks, that helped them to overcome such astonishing odds. Peter Schmeichel, though, was a Danish hero amongst heroes in that tournament of almost thirty years ago, conceding just four goals in five games to help secure his country victory.

Another first was Manchester United's treble of 1999; no English team had ever managed to achieve the triple triumphs of FA Cup victory, League Championship and European Cup. Again, there was a degree of luck about the achievement. United had seemed destined to go out of the FA Cup at the semifinal stage, which went to a replay against their great rivals Arsenal. The London side were the better on the night, and when they won a late penalty, it seemed certain that victory was assured. They had already had a goal disallowed for offside, and while United's talismanic outfield player, Roy Keane, had been red carded for a foul of Marc Overmars. But the missed penalty saw the game go into extra time, and there Ryan Giggs scored one of the great goals of all time, beating four opponents on a mazy run from the halfway line before blasting the ball into the roof of the net.

Today Peter Schmeichel is a well-respected pundit. When he offers an opinion, people still listen. They are wise to do nothing more.

The Qualities That Made Schmeichel Great

- Opportunity.
- Natural leadership.
- A loving, caring and very natural upbringing.
- The strength of character to pursue his interest in soccer when his home was not a natural soccer home.
- The good fortune of qualifying for the 1992 European Championships.

When Soccer Came Home

It is generally agreed that English soccer is home to the strongest league in the world, even if not always quite the very best teams. Barcelona, Real Madrid and Bayern Munich probably vie for that title, although the likes of Liverpool, with their strong European heritage, could run them close. The same could be said for Manchester United, maybe the biggest club in the world, and Arsenal which is perhaps the one with the strongest traditions, albeit not in Europe.

The infusion of cash from foreign owners has maybe propelled Chelsea and Manchester City close to that league. Sir Alex Ferguson's famous comment about the 'noisy neighbors' (referring of course to City) perhaps identifies where the traditional strongholds regard these upstarts, a group to which Paris St Germain would probably like to belong. That these recent arrivals on the world stage have provided three of the four teams to contest the last two European Cup Finals perhaps adds weight to the idea that money talks.

England is also the birthplace of soccer both as a forefather of the modern game, and also as the genesis of the sport we see today. Given all of that, added to the fact that soccer remains outrageously popular in

England, is the most played sport in schools and in amateur clubs by a million miles, how is it that the national team hold an embarrassingly weak record on the international stage?

There are many possible answers. Arrogance is one. Remember, the FA, the body which controls English soccer (increasingly along with the Premier League) refused to countenance their team from entering any World Cup prior to the end of the Second World War. It felt that its own competition against Scotland, Wales and Ireland was the true 'world' cup; maybe because it could win that one. And while it is agreed that England were unbeaten on home soil until the Magyars firmly put them in their place in 1953, they had played hardly any nation of note prior to that. Even today, the FA faces heavy and on-going criticism for its lack of inclusivity, its retrogressive attitude to the sport it claims to run, particularly on issues such as race and the women's game. Really, it has taken the players, with their determination to stick with 'taking the knee' to bring racism in sport to the fore, and the FA have been embarrassingly quiet on the subject, rather than seeking to take the lead.

Another possible reason for England's relative failure is attitude. While the rest of the world was catching up fast, focusing on the development of technique and skill, England remained in the 'boot it long, chase it hard' category of soccer playing dinosaurs. To be fair, the English climate dictates this to an extent. With the dominance of cricket as the summer sport, soccer is overwhelmingly played in the Autumn, Winter and Spring months. In a climate in thrall to Atlantic weather systems, rain is the predominant weather during these times, so pitches were, for decades, mostly mud baths. Not the best preparation for learning skills. And Britain lacked the foresight to invest early in indoor facilities, as Europe and indeed Brazil, have done. Or to consider artificial surfaces with any seriousness for a long time. As a result, the youngsters who progressed in the game tended to be strongest athletes, able to run fast and kick the ball long. In their early years, smaller, more skillful players sank into the mire. Given that we will see that a small physique is a common early characteristic among the most elite players, that factor is telling. Even when they made it to the top, players whose skills and techniques might rival those of their European and South American peers were somehow distrusted. How else to explain that players of the ilk of Matt Le Tissier, Alan Hudson, Frank Worthington, Stan Bowles and George Armstrong could not reach double figures of caps? Particularly as most of these were at the peak of their powers during England's 1970s doldrums, when they failed to reach either the 1974 or 1978 World Cup finals.

Although many highly skilled players have now graced the Premier league – Kevin De Bruyne, Mesut Ozil, Ronaldo, Eden Hazard,

Eric Cantona, Paulo Di Canio, Dennis Bergkamp, Thierry Henry, Paul Pogba to name a few, what these players have in common is that they are not English. It seems as though really skillful players blessed with excellent technique still find it hard to become established. Many pundits agree that perhaps the most technically adept and personally skilled English player at the time of writing is Jack Grealish. He holds the ball well, dribbles with pace and effectiveness, can pass and score. Like most modern players, he can also defend and fit into a system. Yet despite this, the English structure appears to be built around a 'classic' English striker, Harry Kane. Yes, Kane is an effective finisher, takes a good penalty and can drop deep and create chances for others. But he is not especially mobile, and to be effective needs the game to be built around him. As for Grealish, he did not even get off the bench in England's opening Euro 2020 game (played in 2021, due to Covid). Nor did he get his chance until very late during the nation's failure to dispatch Scotland during its second outing at the tournament.

Whatever the root cause, the fact remains that England's international success is restricted to a semi-final appearance in the inaugural Nations Cup, a semifinal on home soil in Euro '96 and a World Cup semifinal in 1990.

Apart, of course, from 1966. And the star of the show then was captain and immaculate defender, **Bobby Moore**. Moore was born in Barking, in Essex to the east of London, in 1941. While money did not exactly flow, this baby of the blitz was brought up in a comfortable if small working-class semi-detached house. The name of his childhood street – Waverley Gardens – owed more to the whimsy of council planners than the presence of rose bushes and oak trees. It was lorries rather than lilies that populated those 'gardens'.

Moore's progress as a youngster was steady rather than spectacular. He captained his primary school soccer team, Westbury Primary School, and was picked out as the sort of reliable lad who could lead the Barking Primary Schools representative side of his time. He achieved the same sort of success for the area senior schools. Moore played for his local boys' club, South Park Boys, and went on to represent Essex Boys. He recalled losing a cup final at the age of 12, and like many youngsters at that age, thought it was the end of the world. His parents, sensible and solid, showed him that it wasn't. So, Moore's childhood exploits were good enough, but nothing out of the ordinary for any future professional. Certainly, at that stage, there was little to mark Moore out as a boy with exceptional potential.

In fact, those were tough times for Moore. He was a bright lad and passed the 11+, the deeply divisive test which determined so many children's futures – a scheme designed to promote social mobility, but which achieved exactly the opposite outcome. So, success was unusual for a boy from his working-class neighborhood. It meant that his trip to the nearest school for those who passed, Tom Hood Grammar in Leyton, was long and lonely. None of his best mates would join him there. He took a long time to settle, but despite his difficulties at the Grammar, and the sadness of that cup final, he was spotted by a scout with connections to West Ham. It would take, though, an early and lasting supporter of Moore to turn a middling report into something suggesting concrete promise.

Indeed, that mentor - his sports teacher, Tom Russell – was Moore's greatest advocate. It was his glowing reports which first reached the ears of the local scout, Jack Turner, who came to take a look. Turner's report was the sort that must have damned many a young lad to a career somewhere else than soccer. 'Looked fairly useful, but wouldn't set the world on fire,' is a damnation with faint praise if ever there was one. But his local club, West Ham United, had just introduced a new youth policy. Tom Russell had a good reputation as a judge of talent, and his opinion carried enough weight to see Moore invited to join the club and train with its youngsters.

That was the first of Moore's lucky breaks, and evidence of a mentor who had faith in the boy. Although, to be fair to Turner, even Bobby himself hardly rated his talents as outstanding. 'Solid, rather than unspectacular,' being his own assessment of his youthful abilities. That relative mediocrity, though, was a spur to him to improve. He'd once been picked as a last-minute stand in for center forward in an area team. His sole contribution had been to bundle the opposing keeper, ball and all, into the net. As was the wont in those days, the goal stood and that earned him more ire from his teammates than if the ref had disallowed it. But it was another lesson learned, another motivating factor in his journey to greatness. In fact, Moore was a good all-round sportsman. He could well have made a name as a cricketer had he chosen that path, representing Essex boys along with another World Cup winner, Geoff Hurst.

Indeed, Moore may not have achieved the heights he managed had he been picked by a wealthier club. Even in the mid-fifties, decades before the overseas billions reshaped the game, the East London side were the poor boys among London's top teams. They could not compete with the Arsenals, the Spurs or the Chelsea teams who knew they could bring in new youngsters as well as seasoned players almost at will. The West Ham Academy was the blueprint for many of today's club academies. It sought to achieve two goals – to bring through players who could make the first team, and to bring on other players sufficiently far to give them a career as a professional. That way, these players could be sold to other teams, seeing a return on the club's investment of time and energy.

And so West Ham stuck with Moore, saw enough in him to believe he could overcome a lack of genuine pace, a relative weakness in the air compared to other center halves of the time. That is why Geoff Hurst would be able to say, many years later, that for any perceived lack of pace, Moore was rarely beaten in a race for the ball, for any thoughts of aerial weakness, he was rarely outjumped. For every claim that he looked good but delivered little, there were countless examples where a pass from Moore created an attack, where bringing the ball out of defense earned a foul and relieved pressure, where his calmness rubbed off on other players, improving them and hence the team.

A much less savory consequence of Bobby Moore's fame occurred in May 1970. The England captain was with his team in South America in the build up to the 1970 World Cup to be held in Mexico. Bogota, in Colombia, to be precise, and they were there to play a warmup match against the Colombian national team. In the hotel in which the team were staying was located a jewelry shop. Several of the players had bought gifts from this store to take back to loved ones in England.

On the night in question, Bobby Moore and teammate Bobby Charlton were looking at the goods on sale but decided that there was nothing which interested them. They left, but were immediately challenged by the shop's assistant, Clara Padilla. Chaos ensued, with the England players declaring their innocence of the theft of a bracelet of which they were accused by the assistant. They even offered to be searched. Eventually, the matter seemed to be resolved, and apologies were given by the authorities to the English players.

The game was played, and the England team moved on to their final warm up match which was against Ecuador. From there they planned to fly to Mexico for the finals themselves, which would include a stopover back in Bogota. It was while the team were waiting for their connection, watching a film in the same hotel they had used earlier, that two plain clothes detectives walked in and arrested Moore. Apparently – and perhaps as further evidence that the whole matter was a scam for publicity on behalf of the Colombians - the arrest had been intended to take place at Bogota airport, until the British ambassador in Bogota stepped in.

Apparently, a new witness had come forward and said that Padilla had been correct, and Moore had taken the necklace. It turned out there was history of this kind of allegation taking place. A Brazilian team staying at the hotel had suffered the same fate, with this time jewelry being planted among their possessions before demands for money to hush the matter up were issued. The case became a farce, with Padilla claiming that the England captain had placed the bracelet in the pocket of his blazer, which he was able to prove had no pocket. The owner of the shop demanded £6000 in compensation, a fortune in those days, but could offer no clear evidence of the value of the supposed necklace – probably because it did not exist. In the end, Padilla ran out of the court room in tears, and the whole matter was exposed as a scam, albeit one which harmed England's preparation for their attempt to retain their trophy.

It is not just Moore from this list of greats whose fame has generated malicious claims and rumors. As well as genuine ones. As we will see shortly, both George Best and Diego Maradona fell foul of the law after their prime. Lionel Messi was sentenced to 21 months in prison for tax fraud, although that was changed to a fine. The former model, Kathryn Mayorga, allegedly claimed compensation of £56 million from Cristiano Ronaldo after accusing him of raping her. Ferenc Puskas was even alleged to have been killed fighting against invading Soviet Forces. It seems as though dealing with false claims and inaccurate news is another burden to be borne for being in the public eye.

Historic Britain is littered with the blue plaques marking a house in which one of its history's finest names has lived. Given England's obsession with soccer it is perhaps a surprise that until recently not one soccer player's home had been honored by such an accolade. It is also the case that the majority of these blue plaques adorn splendid houses, the sort occupied by men and women already rich, even if they are still to achieve their greatest fame. Maybe that explains the long-time absence. Britain's leaders like to speak highly of their working-class people but do little to actually celebrate them. What one doesn't expect is to walk down a street of fairly small, very ordinary semi-detached homes and see such a plaque. Then again, it could not be more fitting that the first of these to go to a soccer player should adorn the wall of the house in which Robert Frederick Moore grew up.

The Qualities That Made Moore Great

- A determination to work hard at the game, to overcome his limitations.
- The mental strength to overcome the challenges of being displaced, educationally, at the age of 11.
- The determination to prove people wrong.
- A strong sense of right, leading to excellent leadership skills.

- A mentor who believed in him and ensured that he was given the chance to train at West Ham United as a boy.
- The good fortune to be caught up in his club's excellent new youth development policy.

Soccer's Playboy

To be a Cobblers fan in the 1960s and 1970s. The East Midlands team, Northampton Town, to give them their proper name, managed to achieve the remarkable feat of going from the bottom division of the English League – Division Four as it was known then – all the way to the top table, then back again with such momentum that they could not stop themselves from plummeting downwards and facing expulsion from the league a decade after their rise began. They finished towards the bottom of the fourth division in 1971-72 and in those days, the lowest four clubs of that division and the top from the next tier down (the Southern League and Northern Premier League back then) would have a kind of election whereby league clubs would vote to elect which of the teams could compete in the next season's fourth division. Fortunately, for Cobblers' fans, Northampton secured enough votes to retain their place.

Northampton had, in those days, a remarkable ground. Probably, the only two and a half sided professional soccer stadium in Britain, maybe the world. The problem was, their ground was owned by the Northamptonshire County Cricket club, and one side of the pitch was the boundary line of the cricket pitch. Fans who liked to stand on the 'cricket side' could reach across the rope and touch their heroes as they took a throw in. If they wanted to. Opposite that open side was a normal stand, and behind one goal the most decrepit of terraces, called the Hotel End, after a hotel in which nobody in their right mind would ever stay. The other goal was home to the Kop. An open topped half stand which extended from behind the center of one goal to the corner flag. Next to it stood a bowls club, and it was not unusual for fans sitting in the few seats high enough to see to spend more time watching the elderly crown green bowlers than the Cobblers. A cheer would emanate when the ball was returned by one of the aging sports players following a wayward shot.

But this is not a chapter about Northampton Town (although, interestingly, their habit of playing in uncompleted grounds continues. Some financial issue befell them midway through building a new stand at the Sixfields ground in which they now play, and it remains, years later, uncompleted, a structure without seats.)

Yet in 1970 an unusually full County Ground saw the Cobblers host Manchester United in the fifth round of the FA Cup. It was rare for Northampton to reach such heights, and to welcome the likes of World Cup winner Bobby Charlton and, of course, **George Best**.

George Best was never far from controversy. On that early February day, he was returning from a four week ban for kicking the ball out of a referee's hand. He was full of pent-up aggression and was determined to put on a show. Suffice to say, United won 8-2 and Best scored six. Afterwards, he uttered perhaps the most understated words of any soccer player in the history of the game. 'I don't really class myself as a footballer,' he said. Although, he did put his comment in a bit of context. 'I call myself an entertainer. I know a lot of people have paid me to see me do something spectacular and that's what I was trying to do on Saturday. It's my job to do something that will send people away feeling that they'd like to see me play again.' A wish which probably didn't extend to the Northampton Town players.

George Best was born in Belfast on the 22nd of May 1946. His parents were hard working, and money was tight. For Best, though, he recalls a happy childhood, if a slightly lonely one. With mum and dad out at work, he spent a lot of time being looked after by his grandparents.

His favorite one, Grandad Withers, died on the day he took his 11+. His parents kept the news from him, lest it should impact on his performance. Evidence, surely, of caring parents. Best recalls going into a shop as he headed for school, and the news was clearly already known in the community. The boy thought the shopkeeper asked him when his Grandad was getting married. Only later did he realize she had said 'buried'. Best recalls being devastated by the news; maybe that influenced his view of the grammar school he won a place at by passing the 11+ test.

He hated it. Echoes of Bobby Moore in that, a young boy being distanced from his community by educational success. Mostly, though, he disliked the school because they did not play football there. Best played truant almost from day one. He'd hide in the toilets until his classmates had returned to lessons, then go out to play soccer for the afternoon, usually by himself using a tennis ball.

Maybe there was an insight into his character, though, by what he did when he tired of his solitary soccer game. He would shoplift, although small stuff like pens and pencil sharpeners. Not that he needed the items, and indeed he thinks a part of him wanted to get caught in the act, to bring some attention to himself. Attention seeking seemed something that would dominate his later life.

He would try to skip school by appearing ill. His favorite trick was to suck red wine gums, to make his tonsils look red and sore. It backfired. So convincing were his actions that he was eventually sent to hospital to have his tonsils taken out.

Eventually, he was deemed an unsuitable candidate for a Grammar School education and was sent to a local secondary school. At least they played soccer there, and that suited the talented teenager. Although he took a dim view of academic matters, Best's commitment to his soccer was second to none. He rarely received criticism, largely because he could do anything with a football, although once his manager of the time, Bud MacFarlane of Gregagh Boys' Club, told him his left foot could be stronger.

Best practiced incessantly for the next week, then played his next match wearing a plimsoll on his right foot and refusing to use it in the game. Apparently, he scored 12 goals with that booted left foot, in a 21-0 victory.

The theme of timing which seems to be a common thread among the greats we have covered once more plays a role in the rise of George Best. In 1958, the Busby Babes were the most promising team in Europe. Led by the iconic Sir Matt Busby (minus the 'Sir' back then), this group of youngsters threatened to enable Manchester United to dominate the continent. At the time, they were on course to secure their third successive league title and had just progressed to the semi-final of the European cup after defeating Red Star Belgrade. It was February 6th, 1958, and the smallish plane in which they were flying home from Belgrade stopped off at the Munich Riem airport in West Germany to refuel before completing the remainder of its journey. Two attempts were made to take off from Munich, but there seemed to be a problem. A boost surge in one of the plane's propellor driving engines. The pilot had to make a choice; abandon the journey and return to England the following day or give it another go. By now snow was falling and a buildup of slush was adding a further problem. The pilot made the decision to give it one more try, but that slush slowed the Airspeed Ambassador down on the runway. It could not get up enough speed to take off, and by the time the pilot realized, the slush prevented the plane from stopping on the runway. It ploughed into a fence, tearing off a wing and killing twenty three of the forty-four passengers on board.

The Busby Babes were decimated.

So it was that three years later Matt Busby was still attempting to rebuild the team. He was approached by a scout who had seen a young, slim Irish boy whose talents seemed extraordinary. 'I think I've found you a genius,' wrote the scout.

The boy had been on the books at Glentoran, but was let go, his coaches sensing that he was just too small and lightweight to cope with the physical challenges of the game. In stepped Manchester United, and a legend was created. Although not straight away. On his first journey to Manchester, Best became homesick and returned to Northern Ireland after just two days. He was soon back. Best, wily, willowy, was soon terrifying full backs as he slid up the wing, as soft and slippery as silk. He made his debut at just 17 years and would spend the next eleven years becoming an icon at Manchester United.

He was not the only great player at United in that era. Busby built another wonderful side, creating it around the genius of Best, alongside Bobby Charlton and Denis Law. These three became known as the United Trinity. The regained the title in 1965 but it was on the European stage where Best secured his legendary status. The preeminent side of the time were Benfica, Eusebio to the fore. Best destroyed them in Lisbon, scoring twice in the opening thirteen minutes. He was still a teenager at the time. The larger-than-life winger landed back in Manchester wearing a huge smile and a bigger sombrero. The press had their man. It was the swinging sixties. Youth was the world. England won the World Cup, the Beatles were conquering their own, musical, planet. London was out, the industrial north – Liverpool, Manchester, Leeds – the place to celebrate. In George Best, the media had the sort of flamboyant figure they would grow to adore. In 1968 the winger enjoyed perhaps his greatest year. He scored in the both the semifinal and final of Europe's biggest competition, his strike in extra time of the final proving to be the winner against the still magnificent Benfica team. Later, he was crowned as European Player of the Year. Earlier, he had been the youngest ever recipient of the Football Writers Associated Footballer of the Year award in England.

Best is remembered for two things in equal measure. His on-field genius and his off the park excesses. In that respect, perhaps he was the first soccer player to find himself exposed to the intrusive eye of a media interested in his private life as much, if not more, than his professional one. He was just twenty-two and probably, at that time, the finest individual player in the world. Even Pele sat behind him in that list. Timing would strike again, but not this time with positive results. Following the European triumph, Manchester United slipped. Busby stepped down, and United's recruitment fell apart. 'I increasingly had the feeling that I was carrying the team at times on the pitch,' the Irishman recalled later. The season after his exploits at Northampton Town disciplinary issues began to blight his career further. He was fined by the FA – never an organization to have any time for a maverick – after being booked three times for misconduct. More worryingly, United suspended him for two weeks after he missed the train south for their league match against Chelsea. The reason? He was shacked up with the actress Sinead Cusack. The small lad from Belfast was enjoying his celebrity status. Still though, he could win a game on his own. He often did and was United's leading scorer for six consecutive seasons. But he was attracting more and more attention away from the soccer pitch – on field, his disciplinary problems continued as he was sent off against Chelsea, off field he received death threats on the one hand (in the days before such outrageous acts were considered par for the course for leading soccer players to bear) and was in trouble once more when he failed to turn up for training for a whole week, having closeted himself away with Carolyn Moore, a Miss Great Britain. The celebrity life continued to dominate as he was surprised by Eamonn Andrews who hosted the popular TV show, This is Your Life. Not many sportsmen in just their mid-twenties were given such an honor.

He was a mere 26 when he announced, for the first time, his retirement from soccer. However, come the beginning of the next season, he was back in training. Meanwhile, United was a team in turmoil. The old guard, such as Best, had little to do with the new players at the club, and such a fractiousness in a dressing room is a recipe for disaster. Best himself continued to be distracted by off field events. During Christmas of the 1972-73 season Best, who should have been at the peak of his powers, abandoned training and spent time in London night clubs. Frank O Farrell, the manager at the time, could never get the sort of commitment out of his star man that the great Sir

Matt Busby had achieved. He suspended Best and put him up for sale. But the genius was damaged goods, and nobody was prepared to meet his valuation of £300000. He announced his retirement for the second time but was back at the club just in time for the end of the season.

By 1973-74 Tommy Docherty was in charge. The dour Scot could do no more with the wayward genius that was George Best than his predecessor. By now lack of fitness caused by poor training and a lifestyle not conducive to a professional sportsman was taking its toll. Matters reached their nadir as the year turned that season. He played against Queens Park Rangers on New Year's Day 1974, being part of a team that lost 3-0. Then, he failed to turn up for training (claiming later he had been given leave by the club) and, determined to be tough, Docherty dropped him. Then, matters took an even bigger turn downwards when he was arrested for stealing a passport, a cheque book and a fur coat from the American actress and beauty queen Marjorie Wallace, charges that were all subsequently dropped. But it was the end of the road for Best. Having scored 179 goals in 470 appearances for United, his contract was cancelled at the end of the season. One in which, incredibly, the mighty Manchester United were relegated. At 28, his career turned out to be effectively over.

There was something about Best which put clubs off of him. Perhaps he was considered to be too disruptive in the dressing room; perhaps the alcoholism that would taint, and eventually end, his life prematurely was already too big a problem. But surely, a player who was still one of the country's finest on his day was worth more than a place at the South African Club, Jewish Guild? Or Dunstable Town? Or Stockport County. Or Cork Celtic. By 1976, he had found a little more stability by following so many big names out to the US, where he scored fifteen goals in 23 starts for Los Angeles Aztecs. A brief resurgence followed as he spent a season at Fulham, scoring eight times in 42 matches, before he headed back to the Aztecs, then on to Fort Lauderdale Strikers before joining the San Jose Earthquakes, via a brief spell in Scotland with Hibernian. Nowhere could he settle. Between 1982 and 84, when he finally retired for the last time, he represented Sea Bee and Hong Kong Rangers, Bournemouth, Brisbane Lions, Osborne Park Galeb, Dee Why FC, Nuneaton Borough and finally, ignominiously Tobermore United in Northern Ireland. In fact, after leaving United, he moved eighteen times in ten years.

As a teenager, he had been a quiet boy, one who enjoyed playing snooker in his free time. But then alcohol caught him and ruined him. Whether it was the booze that destroyed his career, or his career that turned him to alcohol, we cannot say for sure. Probably a bit of both. It led to arrest – once in the US when he took money from a stranger's purse when she went to the toilet. 'We were sitting in a bar on the beach,' Best recalled, 'and when she got up to go to the toilet I leaned over and took all the money she had in her bag.' That was to fund his next rounds of drinks. Alcohol led to his imprisonment in 1984 for drink driving. And in 1990, he famously appeared on a prime-time TV chat show, Wogan, blind drunk. Later, he admitted 'I was ill, and everyone could see it but me.'

In fact, Best was physically as well as emotionally damaged. His liver began to fail, and after being admitted to hospital with pneumonia in 2001, he had a liver transplant, nearly dying in the process. He was soon back to alcohol, and in February of 2004 was once more in trouble for drink driving, this time being banned for 20 months.

Maybe today Best would have received more support, more help with the mental and emotional problems that led him to drink. Although, whether he could respond to such help is another question altogether. Back then, though, the former soccer genius who turned playboy once more became the target for media attention. This time, not to celebrate him but to deride him. Perhaps, he was the first sportsman whose iconic status was both created by the press, before being destroyed by the press.

For Best, though, it was always his soccer that was by far the more important consideration than his lifestyle. 'I don't give a toss about anything else,' he once said. 'As long as they remember the football. If only one person thinks I was the best player in the world, that'll do for me, because that's what it was all about as far as I'm concerned.'

Maybe in that quote we can find another reason to suggest why the genius with a soccer ball saw his own career implode. Perhaps it was not just a love of excess that drove him to drink. Some argue that Best's own standards were so high that in fact he could not live up to them. And that, very significantly, nor could Manchester United. That his own desire to be the best in the world saw him put huge pressure on himself, and that therefore it was soccer that drove him to drink, rather than drink being the catalyst of his self-destruction.

If George Best might not emerge as the absolute top player among this group of remarkable performers we have gathered for our book, then a case can certainly be made that he was the most brilliant of them as a young player. Signed by Manchester United at fifteen, debut at seventeen – and remember, Manchester United was not only a huge club, but these were the days when players often waited until later to make their debuts in the biggest of teams.

Scored on his second outing before going on to play an outstanding role in taking United to the top of the domestic and European trees, winning the Ballon d'Or in the process. All that by 22. In fact, Best knew that his strongest years were still to come. One of his biographers, Duncan Hamilton, says that in his own mind Best thought he would reach the peak of his talents around the age of 29. Youthful dreams that may seem from the perspective of today. But maybe it was not Best himself who went off the rails, but rather Manchester United.

It is a truism that one man cannot make a team. Best had to, and incredibly almost achieved such an impossible aim, because United really did begin to go downhill as the 1970s dawned. Slowly at first, but with gathering and unstoppable momentum. Recruitment was poor, and leadership was lacking. For a perfectionist like Best that was a major problem. He was never a man – or a boy for that matter – to accept inadequacy in others. Gradually, he found himself surrounded by it. For a while, he was able to retain his own impossibly high standards in the midst of mediocrity. He remained obsessed by the sport and retained that desire to run with the ball just as he had both as a boy and as a youngster breaking into the United side. Despite the idea that he lost interest in the game, those who knew him well insist that this was not the case.

If the match was going well, he wanted it to last forever. If his own performance was below his own high standards – and they were so great that often it was – then he wanted to continue playing until he could address his self-perceived failings. Even as his career was beginning to collapse, he was still the finest player in the country, maybe even Europe or the world. It was just that his United team were no longer able to perform to the standard they, including Best, had set. It was something the great man could not get his head around, and with which he could not cope.

The additional problem was that, contrary to popular perception, George Best was not a lowly paid soccer player while still a young man. He was extremely rich, and because of the tax situation in the UK at the time, took much of his income in cash. The rumor goes that his cleaner once found £30000 stuffed into a sock she was about to put through the washing machine. Every one of our greats held a degree of obsessiveness. That is inevitable in anybody who works so hard to reach the top of their profession. Best had such obsessiveness in abundance. To be surrounded by ready cash was without doubt a temptation too far for the young man.

Certainly, it is true that the biggest salary he received from Manchester United was £250 per week, and that was right at the end of his career when everything was going wrong. But while earning through endorsements was not widespread in the 1960s and 1970s, it did happen. If you were good enough to earn it. That meant being a popular personality, certainly. But also being a great player... or actor or musician. Just how great George Best was can be revealed in the fact that that he was drawing at least £100000 a year from those endorsements by the turn of the 1970s. A figure which is the equivalent of close to £1.5 million today. And in an era when sponsorship was very, very unusual.

That, in itself, is a marker as to just how astonishing a soccer player was George Best. It is one as clear as watching the wily dribbler leave defenders for dead or finishing a move with a deadly strike. Even, as his Manchester United team increasingly fell short of his own exacting standards, both creating the chance and putting it away. Alone. We should never lose sight of such brilliance, despite all of the murk and mayhem that surrounded his later career.

We have to come back to that soccer match at Northampton Town's County Ground. Maybe that Best scored six of United's eight on that day was an early indicator of what was to come. A sign that his team, if not yet descending the slippery slope, were nevertheless peering down into the abyss and deciding which way to turn.

As we have said, he wanted to be remembered as an entertainer. Somebody who lit up a soccer pitch, who thrilled the crowd, who even drew a gasp of admiration from opposing players and fans. To have seen him, slim, balanced and so, so agile, leaving his defenders lunging at air, trailing in his wake was to have witnessed soccer as entertainment at a level never before, or after, bettered.

It is just so sad that, for whatever reason, he could not have thrilled the world for longer.

Best was only 59 when he died, his life of excess finally catching up with him. 'I know what people will think,' he said only weeks before succumbing on the 25[th of] November 2005 to infections related to his transplanted liver. 'They'll forget all the rubbish when I'm gone, and remember the football, simple as that.' We can only hope he was right.

The Qualities That Made Best Great

- A supportive, extended family.
- A passion for soccer above all else.
- A small frame as a child, which encouraged him to perfect skills and techniques in order to cope.

- A love of entertainment and being the entertainer. A little like Ronaldo.
- The fortitude to get over the death of his grandfather at a vulnerable age.
- The strength to return to England after homesickness sent him home to Northern Ireland.
- A great mentor in Sir Matt Busby, along with arriving at United as they were beginning to re-grow their team.

To be fair, these qualities were perhaps less developed in Best than in the other greats in this book. Maybe that was why his time at the top was similarly curtailed.

The Boy from the Estate

'I'd rather have your sister than your shirt,' the unpleasant words uttered by Marco Materazzi to **Zinedine Zidane** in the heat and pressure of extra time of the 2006 World Cup final. Niggles had been on-going between the two throughout the game after the Italian boss, Marcello Lippi, instructed the Inter Milan defender to mark the French star.

Zidane reacted to the words, headbutting the Italian in the chest. He must have caught as big a nerve as the metaphorical one the Italian had hurt with his sexist, offensive and sexually harassing comment. Materazzi fell as though pole-axed although the impact could not have been any more unsettling than the many crosses the defender had cleared with his upper body over the years.

'I wasn't expecting it in that moment. I was lucky enough that the whole episode took me by surprise because if I had expected something like that to happen and had been ready for it, I'm sure both of us would have ended up being sent off,' boasted the Italian some years later. Big man. Zidane was, of course, sent off. Whether the referee, Horacio Elizondo, heard Materazzi's comment, or understood it, is unknown. We have to give him the benefit of the doubt. He did at least consult his linesman. However, it is clear from Zidane's reaction that something was said to him. As with racism, any form of discrimination or harassment can only be tackled if it is punished more severely than the reaction it causes. Instead, on this occasion, sexism handed the Italians advantage in the World Cup final.

Fortunately, although the world was temporarily outraged by Zidane's actions, and he was disappointed himself with what he did, the French fans forgave their hero quickly. Rightly so, because the shaven headed attacking midfielder is one of the finest players not only in French soccer history, but that of the world.

Zinedine Zidane's father was destitute. He worked as a casual laborer on building sites, was often homeless, and it was only later, when he was married, with five children, that he was able to begin to settle down. The youngest of those five children was Zinedine, or Yazid as he preferred to be known. But even though the family now had a home - they lived in a small, crowded apartment in the North Marseille housing estate known as La Castellane - they had little else to call their own. La Castellane was a relatively new estate when Zinedine was growing but it was tough. Built in the late sixties for refugees from the Algerian War which ended in 1962, it quickly garnered an unwanted but deserved reputation for hardship, for drug use, prostitution and as a hotbed for poverty induced crime.

People from La Castellane were considered bad news by the local populace of Marseille, and it was bad news to be forced to grow up in La Castellane.

As is so often the case in communities where money is scarce, boredom lay behind much of the criminal enterprises into which the young were drawn. There was little to do. The Algerian community was unpopular not only in Marseille, but France as a whole back then. For young kids, like Zinedine, there was only one thing to occupy their time, other than engage in criminality. Play soccer. Since Zinedine's parents were upright members of their challenged community, they did everything they could to keep him on the straight and narrow. Not that such a worthy outlook sheltered the young from all the dangerous influences around them. For extra protection, Zinedine had his sister, Noureddine, with whom he held a close relationship. She looked after her little brother, made sure he was not drawn into the criminal underworld which existed all around them. In fact, that criminality was not even an underworld. It was opaque, present and obvious. Noureddine protected her brother from its tentacles. Thus, when

Materazzi uttered his unpleasant words, they struck home much harder than might have been expected.

That urge to protect was built into Zidane from an early age. Often, he would be sent home from school for standing up – physically – for a friend. As he got older, it would be soccer pitches from which he was expelled, this time for standing up for teammates.

Maybe that side of his character comes as a surprise, because Zinedine's father, Smail, and his mother, Malika, were kind people, calm and measured. Meanwhile, the youngest member of the family was getting noticed. He began to make his way through teams, the concourses between the concrete tenements of his early years being replaced by patches of rough grass, and then proper pitches, and finally surfaces of good quality. The rough T shirts and shorts he wore as a small child changed to proper soccer shirts, and the full soccer kits.

But although young Zinedine was a technically gifted player, he seemed to be one of contrasts. Quiet, shy almost, he also carried at times a dominant personality on the pitch. Always the highest achiever in any assessment of technical prowess, he frequently made little impression in matches.

At a time when French soccer was beginning to attract huge investment, and teams were seeking to build and develop their youth networks, nobody seemed interested in the poor kid from La Castellane. This was a surprise to his coaches, who knew what Zinedine could do, but somehow, he made little impression on the scouts who came to watch.

Perhaps that was because of his slight physique. In fact, although it was undetected when he was a child, Zidane suffered from a rare form of anemia. It made him tired, and sometimes even lethargic. His parents had very little, but they were paying whatever they had to help their son with professional coaching and to go on fee charging courses, but they could not make him grow, or fill out.

It wasn't until he was 14 that the boy's luck changed. Jean Varraud, a coach from AS Cannes, had come down to look at a particular player in a regional U15 tournament. The boy he had come to see was not picked to play, but instead he saw a technically gifted but very small and light young boy, one who seemed to hold a passion for soccer more than a passion for winning at any cost.

He asked around, and soon discovered that nobody had spotted the potential in the boy. Astonishing. 'He has hands were where his feet should be,' the talented and committed scout said later. But there were problems. He seemed such a gentle soul, and one who could surely be easily led by harder, tougher and more worldly cynical kids from his estate. Yet being the youngest played well for Zinedine. He had the most caring of parents, three brothers and a sister who looked out for him. Nobody was going to mess up Zinedine Zidane. Or mess with him. And now he had a mentor, a scout with a passion for finding the best young players around, and for giving them the best chance of stepping into the boiling pot of professional soccer.

The parallels between Zidane and that other great, Johan Cruyff, bear some examination. As players they were similar, multi skilled performers each with excellent technique. Perhaps Zidane was the more emotional of the two – his temper could occasionally get him into trouble, and that encouraged opponents to wind him up. Both were fine dribblers; each had an eye for a defense splitting pass and the technique to deliver it. Both were cool, collected goal scorers who also possessed the ability to unleash a rocket in their arsenal. Whilst if categorizations are relevant, Cruyff might be defined as a striker, whereas Zidane was more of a midfielder, Cruyff's advocacy of total football saw the two players effective in similar parts of the pitch. Indeed, each could grace the number 10 role in any team – international or club – in the history of the game. It was as coaches, though, that their talents are best compared. If Cruyff was a superstar at Barcelona, where of course he also played, then so was Zidane at the Catalan's rivals, Real Madrid. Having been a star on the pitch for Los Blancos, he became their coach in 2016, having been appointed assistant to Carlo Ancelotti in 2013. Thus began an incredible succession of Champions League trophies, firstly in 2014 and then, following Zidane's move to the top job, further titles were secured consecutively from 2016 to 2018. If Cruyff's status at Barcelona is set in stone, then Zidane's is at least cast in bronze.

Despite this, his reputation as a coach still sits some way behind his achievements as a player. Having broken into the AS Cannes first team as a sixteen-year-old, he moved to Bordeaux in 1992. It was there that his name became more widely known, and he was selected for the talented French national team in 1994. Next, it was the Italian giants Juventus, before he made the move across Europe to Spain, to play for Real from 2001 to 2006. The transfer for that move, at 77.5 million euros, remained a record for another eight years. At just 34, so young for a modern era player, Zidane hung up his boots relatively early. Stop while you are at the top. It's a good basis by which to live any life.

Zidane's trophy cabinet must rival any of the greats examined in this book, including at club, international and individual level. He won the UEFA Intertoto Cup with Bordeaux, a feat he repeated with Juventus, and secured three league titles, two at Juventus and one at

Real Madrid. At Juventus he was twice a runner up in the Champions League, before finally lifting the trophy as a player with Real. He won Super Cups with both Juventus and Real Madrid, as well as an Intercontinental cup with the Spanish side.

With France he secured a winners' and a runners up medal in the World Cup, plus a European Championship title. His list of personal awards would fill a book in themselves. Included among these are a Ballon d'Or, won in 1998, and the Golden Ball award at the 2006 World Cup: that despite his sending off in the final.

So, in Zidane, we find yet another player who emerged from the toughest of upbringings to conquer the world. Another such player features as our last soccer playing 'great'. In Diego Maradona, though, we discover a player who took idolatry to a completely new and unique level. A man who would become a God to his supporters, a deity to his nation, a hero to the poor, the neglected, the exploited and the abused.

But also, to many, a villain. Maybe Ferenc Puskas could be criticized for abandoning the country of his birth when it fell to Soviet invaders; perhaps George Best's personal demons tarnished his reputation. Maybe even Zidane's headbutt, and occasional displays of petulance, spoiled his reputation. Perhaps even Johan Cruyff's smoking limits his position as a role model to sports players across the world.

Yet none of the above can compare to the mixed feelings people hold towards Diego Maradona. A God and a Devil in equal measures.

The Qualities That Made Zidane Great

- A poor upbringing, and determination to escape the threat of crime on his estate.
- Committed and loving parents, who did all they could to give their son opportunity.
- Supportive, protective and caring siblings.
- The strength of character to overcome physical illness.
- A small frame and physique forcing him to develop technique and skill in order to be able to compete.
- The good fortune to be around as his local club were developing their youth structure, and be spotted by a scout at a tournament.
- Passion and fight.
- A love of the sport. Not just winning, but the aesthetics of the game.

- Incredible determination – to learn and embed skills, to avoid the troubles of his estate, to stand up for others.

The Footballer Who Became a God

'There are many people who are scared to admit that they came from the shanty, but not me, because if I hadn't been born in the shanty, I wouldn't be **Maradona**.'

More than any other soccer great in this book, **Diego Maradona** achieved a status in his homeland close to that of a deity. Maybe, more than close. Among a collection of soccer stars-to-be who began life in the most deprived of circumstances, Diego Maradona topped the poverty league. He was proud of his background, proud of being a child of the streets. It fitted his image; one created and exploited not only by this diminutive powerhouse, but also by those who surrounded him, and lived off his back.

He was equally proud of his first soccer ball. It was a gift from his uncle, for his third birthday, and it was the only proper toy the child had. 'That first football was the most beautiful present of my life,' he said. 'The day I was given it I slept all night, hugging it.'

Dribbling that ball through the rough streets helped the young Diego hone the skills which would later light up the world. Maybe what was more astonishing than even his talent as a young boy was that he managed to avoid falling into serious trouble as a child. (In fact, the worst thing that he did fall into was the family cesspit, where his uncle – the one who gave him the soccer ball present – heaved him from the stinking shit. It turned out to be a metaphor for life for Diego, although, sadly, one that ultimately would not come totally true. The shit would get him in the end.)

The reason that he stayed, just, on the side of right was down to his parents. Tota, his mother, and Chitora had spent their formative years living in poverty in the town of Esquina close to the border with Paraguay. They had grown up as neighbors, married and travelled to Buenos Aires to find their fortunes. They were respected people, known for their upright attitudes and commitment to their faith and family. Although, that morality might be seen as slightly different to the values of the West. It was OK, in their mind, to not pay their taxes, to sneak free rides on the local buses, but not to let down their neighbors or their family or their friends.

But despite their moral integrity, the fortunes they sought were far from accessible. Tota periodically worked in service, being treated as little more than a slave, while Chitora risked his health at the local bone crushing factory. It was only as their son ran about, his ball glued to his feet, that they began to realize that they might be parents not only to a stocky, tough little boy, but one who could be a ticket out of poverty for them. Not in an exploitative way – their love for their son was unquestionable. But anybody would seek to escape from the kind of economic destitution and social discrimination in which they were living in Argentina during the 1960s.

Diego – and his parents' – break came in 1968. Through a neighborhood connection, the eight-year-old was given a trial by Francisco Cornejo. He looked after Cebollitas, which was the youth team of the Argentine first division outfit, Argentinos Juniors. Cornejo was not particularly interested in looking at another kid from the slums. To begin with, at least. But he was persuaded to do so. What he saw appeared to be a freak. How could this incredibly short and astonishingly squat child become a soccer player? A boy whose head seemed so large as to be an afterthought stuck onto his tiny body, as though the shop had run out of the real sized heads and grabbed the nearest one to hand. But the boy could perform wonders with a football.

Cornejo's second impression was that somebody was trying to hoodwink him; that the young Diego was actually much older than the others, which accounted for his broad physique (if not his height), but he checked the boy's identity card, and realized that he was just eight years old.

The problem was that, in Argentina at that time, the moral fiber of Diego's parents might be strong. But their sense of right and wrong was more questionable. Again, at least by Western standards. Those parents were persuaded to take their son away from his studies, and to almost cede parental responsibility for the boy to Cornejo. He could see he had a star on his hands, and the Maradonas were star-struck by the possibilities their son could bring. We should not judge, from our comfortable Western lives, but it seemed as though soccer success was more important to those around Diego, particularly Cornejo, his new mentor, than the boy's well-being. He was injected and given pills to help him grow, these provided by a doctor with a highly dubious reputation who worked, in part, providing illegal drugs to sports players – both in soccer and boxing.

This commercial exploitation of the boy continued throughout his childhood. He even appeared on a popular Argentine TV program, a child prodigy who could juggle bottles as well as balls.

But this is not to belittle the horror of the social inequalities of Argentine society, a concern which drove Maradona throughout his life.

'This kid is going to be the salvation of us all, Dona Tota,' said Cornejo to Diego's mother at one point. He may not have meant it as we interpret the words here, but there was truth in what he had to say.

To be an Indian in Argentina back then was to be the untouchable, an Epsilon to the Brave New World's Alphas. Native Indians were the dregs of society. Argentina was a deeply racist society – even after the reforms of the Perons. The best people where white, of Northern European heritage, people who played polo rather than soccer. Indians were servants, there to be exploited, to be displaced, to be the first victims of any disease which struck the nation. No doubt the poverty associated with this drove the young Maradona as much as his natural love of the game. Twin passions which originated in his parents and were later enhanced by his coaches.

An example came when he was just eleven years old. Such was his talent that he was picked to play in a competition in Uruguay. The other children in the tournament were offspring of the wealthy, children whose parents could buy their inclusion with cash rather than their child's talents. These youngsters were feted and looked after in the middle-class homes of their Uruguayan neighbors. Maradona, the kid from the slums, was put up in a tiny shack without running water – his host a native Indian like himself.

It is easy to criticize Diego Maradona, and he did much in his life deserving of such criticism. But just as with that infamous World Cup quarter final which would later deify and destroy his reputation in equal measure, his story is always complicated; alternately mired in darkness and shining with brilliance.

Where to begin with the diminutive, dynamic Argentine's adult career? The brilliance of his goal against England in that 1986 match, or the other goal, the hand of God goal, which saw him rise and punch the ball blatantly past Peter Shilton, the England keeper? Or the sad sight of this astonishing man, far past his prime, heavy, puffy faced screaming into the camera after scoring in Argentina's win against Greece in the 1994 competition?

That was just three days before he was banned for taking the performance enhancing drug ephedrine. If Zidane's international career ended in an unforeseeable but, maybe, forgivable way, the same cannot be said for this self-abuse which saw Maradona leave the world stage for the final time. In the soccer sense, at least. Simply, what Maradona did was to cheat. Something for which of course he had previous. Although, again, the influence of those around him, whom he trusted and who should have known better, had its part in the creation – and destruction - of this soccer playing demi-God.

In fact, that 1994 tournament is the place to end with any analysis of Maradona's career. To mention, because it has to be said, but then to pass and think back to this little magician's talents. The ball became an extension of his feet when he dribbled, two footed. He was strong as the most powerful bear, full of vision and force. He led wherever he turned, a magnetic – if flawed – personality. A giant who stamped over the game just as it began to dominate the world.

Maybe it was also timing that played a part in Maradona's rise to mythical status. Within his own nation, at least. In 1982, the Argentinian nation had been humbled over the Falklands War. These islands, deep in the South Atlantic, formed an isolated outcrop of the British Commonwealth but were considered a part of Argentina by that nation, which called them Las Malvinas. Argentina landed forces on the islands, and the nearby rocks of St Georgia. The British Prime Minister at the time, Margaret Thatcher, responded as nobody could have predicted, particularly the Argentinians. Rather than negotiating a settlement over the islands, perhaps offering homes back in the UK for the small number of residents who would wish to leave them, she launched a fearsome task force which set sail to relieve the islands. A task force which would cover most of the planet in its journey from north to south, so remote were these islands from the nation which ruled them.

Thatcher was, at the time, a desperately unpopular Prime Minister in Britain, and saw the Falklands as an opportunity to regain favor. Not only with her voters, but in her party as well. Against the might of technologically advanced warships, submarines and aircraft, plus highly trained land forces, the Argentinian army could not compete. Made up mainly of young conscripts, its battalions contained only a tiny proportion of seasoned soldiers. Meanwhile, its navy consisted of little more than the second world war cruiser, the Belgrano, which was famously sunk as it sailed away from the islands. Only the Argentine air force, armed with Exocet missiles, could present a threat to the British armada which sailed south.

Victory was short, swift and savage, and the humiliation for the Argentine junta was felt as much by its people as its military leaders. So, when Maradona put England to the sword four years later at the World Cup, he was transformed from national hero to saint-like status. Maradona represented retribution; revenge in something that mattered almost as much Las Malvinas. Maradona was their savior, their sword of Damocles, thrust down into the soft bellies of the British nation. Such adulation was born and never passed, even as his personal life descended into chaos.

Bill Shankly, great Liverpool coach, once (perhaps apocryphally) stated 'Some people believe football is a matter of life and death…I can assure you it is much, much more important than that.' The quote is often taken out of context, but Maradona's position in the eyes of the Argentinian population, and in particular the poorer elements of that society, supersedes his position as one of the greatest of soccer players ever. Maybe, when it comes to a hierarchy of the greatest players, Diego Maradona sits fractionally under Pele. Many will argue that point. However, when it comes to a soccer player's influence on culture, on freedom and on society none has come close to lifting their people like Diego Maradona. In sporting terms, perhaps only Muhammed Ali, with his fight for the rights of black people in white societies, can run him close.

Diego Maradona died on 25th November 2020 and the world took a collective breath. Some people do carry a kind of immortality. Nelson Mandela perhaps. Steven Hawking. While that is not to suggest that the fabulous but flawed footballer deserved to live in the same league as these world icons, it cannot be denied that he did. If the enormous sense of sadness and shock which echoed around the US, Europe, Australia – anywhere where soccer is worshipped and celebrated – was astonishing imagine how it felt in Argentina.

The distress people felt was genuine, but that Maradona died so young should not really have been so surprising. The little genius was, like George Best (and other soccer players over time) addicted to alcohol. He had abused his body with drugs – cocaine in particular. He had been banned for fifteen months for testing positive for cocaine while playing for Napoli in 1991. He had undergone brain surgery to remove a clot earlier in that November. One can only speculate on the impact of the drugs pumped into his body by the dubious doctor, Cacho Paladino, fifty years before.

Lionel Messi described his hero as 'eternal', saying 'A very sad day for all Argentines and football. He leaves us but does not leave, because Diego is eternal.' The president of Argentina, Alberto Fernandez, even declared three days of national mourning. 'You took us to the top of the world. You made us immensely happy. You were the greatest of them all. Thank you for having existed, Diego. We're going to miss you all our lives.'

When soccer breaks free of its sporting context – which it often does – then Maradona holds the title of the most influential player of all time.

The Qualities That Made Maradona Great

- Abject poverty which he, and his parents, were determined to leave behind.

- A small but very strong frame, which gave him the low center of gravity to develop his skills, and also the need to dominate with more than power alone, because of his lack of height.

- Mentors – his father, uncle and first coach – who were determined to do what it took to make the boy a success. Even if those measures might be considered at times dubious by many.

- A passion and love for the sport. Personal economic circumstances that offered him no alternative to soccer.

- Timing – we cannot call it good fortune, under the circumstances of war – which meant his performances took him from being a worldly genius to a metaphysical one.

Bonus #3:

If you've wondered what separates these greats from the rest, it's not skill or privilege or money. It's a lot more. It's what allows them to bounce back from failure and stay level-headed with success. It's mental toughness. We've actually studied it for the last few years and have published our own book on Soccer Mental Toughness. And, as a reward for staying with us so far, you can get that book for free. Just scan the QR code below to get it.

A Leader Beyond Soccer

Captain of Arsenal. Iconic leader lovingly celebrated in a Nick Hornby classic. The man who takes his team to the fortress that is Anfield during Liverpool's prime. It is 1988. The closest title race ever in English soccer history comes down to the final game. First versus second. Liverpool versus Arsenal. Arsenal need to win 2-0 at the home of the champions if they are to lift the trophy. The prize is more than just a league title. It will be the first championship the club has won in seventeen years, since the days of the double, and Bertie Mee. It will mark the end of a terrible barren spell. Those years broken only by a single FA Cup triumph, and that is nearly a decade back. Tony Adams is the captain who sees his side win that most dramatic of league titles. The winner scored with virtually the final kick of the game. 'It's up for grabs now…' Brian Moore's iconic commentary. Watch it on You Tube. Adams is the man who leads the Gunners. The man who captains his country. The man who bursts through from the back to hammer a fourth past Everton on the final day of another winning season, gets on the end of a through ball sent over his shoulder. Played in by fellow centre half, Steve Bould. Volleys it home.

Donkey. Donkey Adams. Picture in the Sun newspaper. Donkey Adams with donkey ears stitched onto his head. Donkey, donkey. Because apparently, he cannot play. A stopper – no more. A donkey. Those who watch him know the truth.

Arms raised. A statue outside the Emirates Stadium. Mr Arsenal. An entire career played at one club.

Mr Arsenal. **Tony Adams**. Hero to fans. Described by Arsenal's two most successful modern day managers as a 'colossus' and a 'professor of defence'. Icon to a club. Saviour to so many.

Tony Adams. Alcoholic.

Sheffield United. Getting the timing wrong the night before. Waking up. Still drunk. The usual? Don a plastic bin bag, run, sweat the alcohol out of the system. It works in training. Run. Too late. Not with a game later that day. 'I'm not feeling too well boss.' Run.

'Well tried, lad.'

Man of the match. Tony Adams. Mr Arsenal. Alcoholic.

English football has a drinking culture. Arsenal is a club with a drinking culture. Except, that is not the correct term. The word 'culture' implies something good. Something admirable. Until their run to the last four in the 1990 World Cup, English football has not produced a semi-finalist in a major international tournament. Not since 1966. Whilst continental players hone their technique with hours on the training pitch, English players complete their contracted hours, shower, change, get into their Ford Granadas or Capris and head down to the pub. Pint after pint. Night after night. It's what men do. Working class men. If they can afford it. At least, that's the excuse. At Arsenal, in the 1980s and early 1990s, this 'culture' is taken to extremes.

But Tony Adams? The man most responsible for 1-0 to the Arsenal? The 'nil' bit at least. Leader of the team, leader of the strongest back four in English league history? Dixon, Winterburn, Bould and Adams. Seaman in behind. Arm raised as yet another striker strays offside. At Arsenal the advertising hoardings alongside the tight Highbury pitch mark defending zones. Step out, arms raised. Flag rises. Whistle blows. A choreographed routine, worthy of the finest West End musical. The West End. Only three miles distant from Arsenal's hallowed Highbury. You get good pubs in the West End. Good clubs, too.

Those who don't know don't believe it. You can't be that
organised if you spend most of the day down the pub. You can't lead
that team if you half cut most of the time. If you're an Arsenal fan, you
idolise him. If you're an opposing team's fan, you hate him. If you are
a neutral, you admire him. If you are a journalist, one of the privileged
few with access to the nation's leading players, you keep the secret you
must have known. Then, when drinking is so rife, is there a story in
singling out one player? Drinking has destroyed perhaps British
football's most talented soccer playing genius ever, George Best. It
ruined perhaps England's greatest ever natural finisher, Jimmy Greaves.
It cut both their careers short. Is it time to bring down the Arsenal
captain? The England captain. The editors would like it. But even so,
you don't write the stories. After all, drinking is so rife, there might be
more harm in printing the truth than in keeping it secret. Nobody likes
to see their heroes fall. Nobody wants to wield the sword. And nobody
wants to become that fallen icon. Especially not the captain of Arsenal.
The club of the gentry. Herbert Chapman and the mighty, sparkling
marble halls of Highbury.

But then the story cannot be hidden any more. Tony Adams is
about to bring English football into disrepute before, eventually, setting
it (with a little help) onto the path of redemption, a track that leads
ultimately to three semi-finals and two finals of major international
competitions in four attempts. He is going to bring about change that

not only saves the careers of so many elite athletes, but also, in some cases, their lives as well.

If a leader is somebody who can bring about positive change, positive results and positive actions in those around him, then surely Tony Adams is the greatest leader that not only soccer, but sport itself, has ever known. But not yet.

Off-season is the worst. Or, those desperate days when a player is injured. Without the regular commitment to training, the benders can go on for days. Pint after pint. Crashing into bed. Wetting yourself. Waking up, soaked in your own urine, stinking, sick, head throbbing, barely able to move.

Tony Adams was born in the East London town of Dagenham in 1957, joined Arsenal in his early teens and after three years finds himself selected for his first team debut. It is just a month since his 17th birthday. The 2-1 defeat at home to Sunderland will not be his finest day but is part of the learning process. He is made team captain at the youthful age of 21. He plays six hundred and sixty nine times for his club. He helps his team lift four league titles, three FA Cups, two league cups and a UEFA Cup Winners' Cup during that time. Tony Adams arms aloft. Cup in hand. He plays 66 times for England, captaining the side on fifteen occasions. When England step out for the final time at the old Wembley Stadium, playing Germany in 2000, Adams is once again the first in the line.

But for all this, his greatest achievements are still to come. Firstly, conquering the alcoholism that plagued him for most of his playing career, and secondly setting up Sporting Chance. And in doing that, not only saving the careers of afflicted sportsman, current and former, but – and it bears repeating - also saving their lives.

But it is not easy. Not at all. The demons are not just in Adams' head, but in the attitude that prevails. The twisted culture of English working class sportsmen. Because, it is a curiously male thing, and a curiously English one. Consider these words, attributed to a senior former professional player in the English league, and published in a national newspaper around the time of Adam's admission of alcoholism. 'I personally do not think there's anything wrong with having a few pints after a game,' says the anonymous player. 'I used to think that if I'd worked hard during the week and ran my socks off on a Saturday, I deserved a pint…There was no need to be a hermit as long as you keep the drink to a moderate amount.'

Notwithstanding the underlying misconceptions of the statement above, those last words were part of the problem for Tony Adams. He could not keep it to a moderate amount. The underlying reasons are no different to those of so many alcoholics, and indeed addicts of many forms. Lack of self-esteem, self-loathing, and strangely that peculiar combination of supreme confidence on the pitch with a lack of personal belief off it. It is hard for those who are not professional sports players to understand this.

In early 1990 he drives his car into a wall. He is breathalysed and found to be four times over the drink driving limit. In December of that year, he is sentenced to four months in Chelmsford prison, serving half that time.

The experience gives lie to the popular notion that a short sharp shock can solve a problem. Adams comes out and returns to drinking. When a new Arsenal manager is appointed, Bruce Rioch, Adams is open that he is probably responsible for his new boss's rapid sacking. As he says, if the team captain is down the pub instead of at training, the manager is at a serious disadvantage. Always one, now, to admit his failings, to face up to his mistakes, Adams has apologised to his former boss.

He accepts he was an alcoholic for twelve years, and for all but the final six months of that time, he has no wish to give up. In one interview he admits that, as much as he would like to do so, he cannot kill himself and the alcohol provides an alternative. On one occasion, when drunk, he crashes down a flight of stairs, requiring 29 stitches in his head. On the pitch he is focussed, in control, but it is the nature of being a professional sports player that there is a lot of down time. Tony Adams cannot cope with that.

Then, slowly, it dawns on this great sporting leader that he needs to do something. He makes that first enormous step - a plea for support – for the first time in his adult life asking for help. He attends Alcoholics Anonymous, a support group, and in 1996 his life changes. He has been sober for just six weeks, when Arsenal appoints one of its greatest ever managers, a man who will address, tackle and change the culture of English football; Mars Bars give way to broccoli; beer to hydration drinks; a culture of silence to a culture of openness. In Tony Adams, Arsene Wenger has a leader, a captain and a convert to promote his new ways, even if the player is a tad sceptical at the outset. In Arsene Wenger, Tony Adams has a man whose outlook helps him to stay sober during the tricky first months.

Yet still we have not reached Tony Adams' greatest achievement. He releases his autobiography in 1998. 'Addicted' takes the sporting world by storm. Never has such a high-profile English footballer been so open about his problems, and his challenges. At first the sporting nation, and particularly the soccer playing parts of it, are in denial. Slowly, it begins to accept the truth. For Adams, trophies, FA Cup and league title doubles follow, and when he hangs up his boots in 2002, he is the most successful captain in his club's history.

A relatively unsuccessful delve into management does follow, but the former player's greatest achievement of all comes when he sets up Sporting Chance, the world's biggest and most successful organisation designed to help professional athletes cope and deal with problems of addiction. Hundreds of professional sports players have benefitted from its support and counselling over the past two decades, and Tony Adams still visits young professionals in a variety of sports, from soccer to cricket to rugby and beyond, offering help, advice and support.

He remains one of the most famous faces in English sport, his reputation one of the strongest, his calm and surprisingly soft voice one of the most reassuring, and his story, especially that from outside the direct influence of the playing field, perhaps one of the greatest.

139

The Qualities That Make Adams Great

- Phenomenal leadership skills
- A passion to bring about change
- Truth and honesty

The Genius Buffeted by the Winds of Change

Soccer is the most popular sport in the world, the most played and the most watched. It evokes the strongest of emotions, enormous highs and impossible lows. There are many possible reasons for this: the speed of transitions; the lack of 'goals' (compare it to, say, basketball); its unpredictability. Surely, though, at the heart of its appeal lies its immense simplicity. Nothing is needed beyond something that can be propelled through being kicked. Therefore, it is a sport that can be played by all, from the biggest to the smallest, the oldest (look at the enormous growth of walking football, for example) to the youngest. From the richest to the poorest.

And therein lies the second reason for its immense popularity. Truly, soccer is the sport of the people. The sport of meritocracy and democracy. So many of its greatest proponents, if not through its entire history, then certainly within the modern game come from the most deprived, impoverished of backgrounds.

This is a situation in which the young **Josef Bican** finds himself. Thanks to the privations caused by a conflict a long way outside of the boy's control. Because Josef is born just prior to World War One, in

September 1913, and by the accident of geography, ends up on the wrong side of that terrible war. Although, of course, it is a time of such outrageous atrocities that it is fair to conclude that nobody ends up on the right side of it.

Whilst hardly wealthy, Josef is not born completely into the poverty he will soon be forced to endure. His mother is Viennese, and his father a Czech from Southern Bohemia. His father is a professional footballer, representing Hertha Vienna. And to complete a sporting pedigree of the highest class, Josef's mother is also a talented athlete, being a competitive runner. But when Josef is just a year old, the war breaks out and his father joins the army. Whilst, unlike many, he survives that terrible event unscathed, physically at least, Josef's father is soon to be faced by a tragic irony. Unharmed by the bullets and bombs of the war, he receives an injury to his kidney while playing football. He does not get it treated as recommended, and, terribly, inconceivably, dies. History does not record why he does not get the injury treated. Maybe it is because an operation is required, and the family lack the money required to pay for this. Or perhaps the prospect of being unable to play for a period while he recovers presents too great a financial risk to his family. He may not earn an income during this time, and with the economic collapse endured by nations such as Austria in the post war years, he decides to try to play through his injury. Whatever, from the age of seven or eight, Josef is fatherless, and the family suddenly face the chronic poverty Josef's father is trying to avoid.

Josef is the middle sibling of three and inherits his father's passion for the game. While his mother takes whatever jobs she can to support her family, he develops the considerable skills which will mark his career while playing street soccer. Such is the poverty facing post war Austria – he grows up on the outskirts of the Vienna, travelling to the Czechoslovakian town of Sedlice for the summers, visiting relatives – that even a city as opulent as his is in crisis. There is no opportunity to wear boots – any shoes he owns are saved for best or necessity – and not even a ball to kick. He and his friends use rolled up socks, or more often, a 'hardrak', a collection of tightly woven together rags. Maybe that is a good thing, because without boots to wear out on the hard roads and pavements, the boys play barefoot.

Which means, of course, there is no room for error. A misplaced foot, a mishit kick, a careless tackle will result in painful bruises, cracks or fractures. Perhaps this is why Josef develops the incisive dribbling skills for which he will become famous, the accurate shooting which will lead him to become one of the greatest goal scorers of all time. Or maybe it is more than that; from his father he inherits the genetic skills of a soccer player; from his mother the determination to work and

143

succeed (even when success is represented by the necessity of keeping a roof over the family's heads and putting food on their table.) From the poverty he endures he develops comradeship, a sense of togetherness with those around him – teamwork, perhaps – and a drive to push himself out of the hand to mouth existence he and his family endure in post war Austria.

But while those attributes are crucial to be successful in any sphere of life, you cannot become a soccer playing superstar with superb skill and excellent technique on determination and ambition alone. It is the street football which hones the amazing talent Josef Bican develops.

And it pays off. As a young teen he begins to turn out for his father's old club, albeit for the second team. He is sponsored at a shilling a goal. Suddenly, a valuable income stream emerges, because young Josef cannot stop scoring. An apocryphal story demonstrates the support his mother gives to her son. Anecdotally, she is watching in the crowd when her son is fouled. She leaps onto the pitch to remonstrate with the offending player, her umbrella playing no small part in the assault. Equally, another unproven story gives truth to the impact of losing her husband to a soccer born injury. This tale says she watched her son only twice during his career, because she cannot bear the memories brought to her mind.

Then, aged just fifteen, Josef makes his senior debut for Schustek. Information about this period is sketchy. Record keeping in this era is variable at best. Schustek are a successful team based in Montenegro these days, but back in the late 1920s they are known as SK Hajduk, have only just been founded, and are yet to find a league in which to play. So, for Josef, it is when he makes his first appearance for the Hertha Vienna first team, aged eighteen, that his career really takes off. He scores more than a goal a game for them and two years later, the goal scorer is representing Austria, and becomes part of perhaps the greatest team in the nation's history. One that reaches the semifinals of the 1934 World Cup, is considered among the finest in Europe, is the first continental side to beat Scotland and earns the pseudonym the 'Wunderteam'.

It is no surprise that aged just twenty-one he is signed up by the most powerful team in Austria, Rapid Vienna, on the for then astonishing salary of 600 schillings. That is more than most working class people could ever hope to earn, if a modest sum by today's standards. The young player from the streets has made it.

Build wise, Josef is like so many second strikers, or inside forwards as they were known back then. He is tank like, as solid as a rock, muscled and agile. His low centre of gravity gives him excellent turning ability, and his control of the ball is excellent. He can change pace in a flash, accelerating away from trouble and through gaps in a floundering defence. He is devastatingly fast, completing the 100 metres in just 10.8 seconds. When Jesse Owens wins the sprint in the 1936 Olympics, he is only half a second quicker. Josef possesses a vicious shot, and those endless days playing on the streets means he is completely two footed. But even at the top of his powers, he continues to practice, practice, practice. A favourite trick is to place bottles on top of the crossbar and hit them one at a time. Rarely does he miss. His short stature leads him to acquiring the nickname Pepi. Then, still in his early twenties he causes shockwaves among the Rapid Vienna hierarchy and fans when he decides to move on to their rivals Admira.

Yet, trouble outside of his control is beginning to present a darkness on the horizon. If Bican's youth was seriously impacted by World War One, then the second conflict becomes as damaging, this time to his football career. Take the 1934 World Cup. This is held in Italy, and it is the hosts who narrowly put out the superbly talented, free scoring Austrians. In the most suspicious of circumstances. It is said that Mussolini, no soccer lover, has decided that the competition will become a propaganda event for his nation. Therefore, they must win the tournament. Using whatever means. By the semi-finals, the pitches are flooded to make rapid passing impossible, and limit the Austrian's teamwork and movement. Further, the Italian goal in their narrow victory is scored when the Austrian keeper is bundled into his own net as he holds the ball. This is not some shoulder barge from a corner, but rather a physical charge which pushes the keeper three metres back and over the line. The referee who allows the goal has apparently been taken to dinner with Mussolini the day before the game.

Then comes the 1938 World Cup. By now Austria has been annexed by the Nazi threat, and firstly it is ordered that only a German team will represent the Axis powers at the World Cup. When it is pointed out that the Austrian team is far stronger than the German side, a bizarre and strictly orchestrated combined team is created, six from one nation, five players from the other. It is no surprise that, with little time to work tactics or develop relationships, the competition is a failure for this hybrid team. In any case, Josef refuses to represent the oppressive regime which has annexed his own country. It will not be the last time he places his conscience above his career. By the time of the next World Cup, which does not occur until 1950, Josef is thirty-six years old, and although still playing, beyond his prime. As are, indeed, the Austrian team.

It is following the arrival of Fascism in Austria that Bican moves to his father's nation of Czechoslovakia. He joins Slavia Prague, remains for eleven turbulent seasons and scores 534 goals in that time. Included here are one twenty-four match season where he nets fifty-seven times, and three separate games when he bags no less than seven. Yet he is never accepted by a significant portion of his teammates and many of the club's fans. It is hard to imagine from today's perspective the distrust and hatred which operated in central Europe during that dangerous time. Hitler's desire to rule the continent. His annexation of Josef's homeland and beyond caused the player to be ostracised and tormented as a poor Austrian in Bohemian Czechoslovakia.

But Josef Bican is made of the sternest stuff, and he stands tall against the discrimination. He applies for Czech citizenship, is awarded it and is able to play for his adopted country's national team. Yet international soccer is basically dead during the war years and the period immediately after it. He manages only fourteen appearances in eleven years, scoring twelve times. He also represents Bohemia and Moravia on one occasion, scoring a hat-trick.

Yet whilst this is happening, Josef's celebrity status is growing. He plays tennis with film stars, dines with the elite of society. He marries Jarmila (they have no children) and enjoys his reputation. In many ways, he moves away from the lessons instilled in him by his hard-working mother. At a time when austerity is all, he lives it up. Then, in 1948, Czechoslovakia becomes communist. As perhaps the biggest name in the nation, he is approached to be the face of the new regime, but, just as he has rejected Naziism, now he rejects communism. He is forced to leave Slavia, a club identified as having a middle class following, regretting that he has turned offers from such European giants as Juventus. Great footballer that he is, Josef Bican is perhaps a touch naïve. In the political sense at least.

He moves to smaller clubs, trying to enhance the working class heritage, which is his true background, despite his time among the nation's elite. Come the May Day parade of 1953, which he is required to attend, once more political events invade his life. Spotted by the crowd they cheer him more than the communist president. Never a wise idea and he is banished once more. He returns to Prague, rejoins Slavia (now known as Dynamo Prague - a Communist decision) and even aged forty-one, returns fifty-seven goals in a season. He retires aged forty-two and enjoys a mixed career as a coach.

However, life as a self-made man under communism is hard. Especially where that man is honourable and refuses to be corrupted. Much of his wealth and property is seized. Sensing the dangers of being regarded as close to an opponent of the communist party, many of his friends turn their back on him. When an event is organised by the International Federation of Football Historians and Statisticians, they decline to include his two hundred and twenty nine goals scored when the world is at war. He and Jamilia refuse to attend the event, drinking coffee from flasks in their hotel room instead. Only later is his true tally allowed (and even that is probably higher, record keeping being poor during the war years and under communism.) When that final total is added up, he is awarded the Golden Boot for being the greatest goal scorer of the 20th Century.

Josef Bican dies in Prague in 2001, aged 88. On the hundredth anniversary of his birth, his beloved Slavia Prague played wearing shirts bearing his signature.

Of all the names in this book, Bican is the one who will be least familiar to most. Astonishingly, his name does not even appear in the Wikipedia page of the Austria National Football Team. Maybe the reason that he is relatively poorly known is because he represents a less than glamorous soccer playing nation; maybe it is because he does not grace the home turf of a leading European or South American club side. Or maybe it is simply because it is the career of Josef Bican, the man full of determination, full of skill and passion, who possesses the most wonderful skills, the most extreme talent. His career, his life even, is hampered by war and political intrigue. That makes things difficult. And so, he is frequently ignored by the media.

But the facts of his career, his goal-scoring record, tells such a different story.

The Qualities That Made Bican Great

- Phenomenal ball skills and control
- Personal drive
- The most supportive of mothers
- The perfect gene set and sporting background

The German Ace

Gerd Müller's name is practically synonymous with goal-scoring brilliance. This legendary figure carved out his legacy in soccer history with an almost supernatural ability to find the back of the net. Born on November 3, 1945, in the small town of Nördlingen, Germany, Müller wasn't always seen as the prodigy he would eventually become. Yet, as time would tell, he was destined to rise above challenges that could have easily derailed his career.

Starting off at TSV 1861 Nördlingen, a local club, Müller's goal-scoring abilities were evident from the get-go. It didn't take long for bigger clubs to notice his talent. In 1964, he made a pivotal move to Bayern Munich, which at the time, was still clawing its way up in the second division of German football. Little did anyone know that this transfer would be a turning point—not just for Müller, but for Bayern Munich as well.

Müller's debut for Bayern in the Bundesliga was nothing short of a spectacle. His physical appearance—stocky and not particularly tall—made some skeptics doubt his potential. But what Müller lacked in physicality, he more than made up for with razor-sharp instincts, lightning-fast reactions, and a knack for intelligent positioning. These qualities made him the focal point of Bayern's attacking strategies, and soon enough, the team began climbing to the summit of German football. By the close of the 1960s, Bayern Munich had emerged as a powerhouse, with Müller solidifying his place as their leading man.

The 1970s ushered in a golden era for both Bayern Munich and Müller. In the 1971-1972 Bundesliga season, Müller accomplished an astounding feat—he scored 40 goals, a record that would remain unbeaten for decades. His goal-scoring wasn't confined to domestic tournaments; on the international stage, Müller was a force to be reckoned with. His prolific scoring propelled Bayern Munich to clinch four Bundesliga titles, four DFB-Pokals, and three European Cups between 1974 and 1976, marking an era of unprecedented success for the club.

But perhaps Müller's finest hour came during the 1974 FIFA World Cup, hosted by West Germany. In a nerve-wracking final against the Netherlands, Müller scored the decisive goal, securing a 2-1 victory for his home country. This goal was the perfect encapsulation of Müller's career—opportunistic, precise, and game-changing. Just four years earlier, in the 1970 World Cup, Müller had walked away with the Golden Boot, having scored 10 goals and solidifying his reputation as the best striker on the planet.

While Müller's on-field exploits were the stuff of legends, his personal life was marred by struggles that few knew about. The pressure to stay on top, coupled with the physical wear and tear of professional football, led Müller down a darker path. After hanging up his boots in 1981, Müller's battle with alcohol dependency began to take center stage, threatening to overshadow his glittering career.

But Müller's story didn't end on that grim note. Concerned for their old friend, Bayern Munich stalwarts like Uli Hoeneß and Franz Beckenbauer stepped in, offering their support and helping Müller get the help he desperately needed. After completing rehabilitation, Müller found a new calling within Bayern Munich, working with the youth teams and passing on his wisdom to the next generation. This phase of his life, characterized by redemption and a renewed sense of purpose, added yet another layer to his already remarkable story.

Müller's contributions to football didn't go unnoticed. In 1970, he received the Ballon d'Or, solidifying his place among the greatest to ever play the game. By the time he retired, Müller had amassed 365 goals in 427 Bundesliga matches and 68 goals in 62 international appearances—a goal-scoring record that still stands as one of the most impressive in the history of the sport.

Gerd Müller's legacy is about more than just numbers and trophies. He challenged the conventional wisdom of what a striker should be, using his intellect and instincts to outsmart defenders. His journey from a small-town boy in Nördlingen to one of football's greatest players is a testament to the power of sheer talent and determination. His influence on the sport is undeniable, and his story continues to inspire new generations of players.

In August 2021, the football community was hit with the sad news of Gerd Müller's passing at the age of 75. Tributes poured in from every corner of the globe, as fans, players, and experts alike honored the man who had left an indelible mark on the game. The statue of Müller outside Bayern Munich's Allianz Arena, depicting him in a familiar celebratory pose, serves as a lasting tribute to "Der Bomber"—a true footballing icon whose legacy will endure for as long as the sport is played.

What set Müller apart wasn't just his goal-scoring prowess, but also his incredible resilience and humility. His story is one of triumphs on the pitch, battles off it, and a legacy that will continue to inspire for generations. When fans look back at the history of football, Gerd Müller's name will undoubtedly stand out as one of the greatest to ever play the game.

The Attributes That Defined Müller:

• Exceptional goal-scoring instincts

• Resilience and determination

• Humility and dedication

The Guardian of Glory

Gianluigi Buffon, a name that resonates with soccer fans worldwide, is universally acknowledged as one of the greatest goalkeepers to have ever graced the field. His story, rich with moments of triumph and tenacity, is as captivating as the man himself. Born on January 28, 1978, in the marble-clad town of Carrara, Italy, Buffon's life is a testament to perseverance, talent, and an indomitable spirit. From a young age, it was clear that Buffon was destined for greatness, but his journey was anything but straightforward.

Buffon's family background reads like a roll call of athletic prowess. With a mother who threw the discus and a father who lifted weights, it was perhaps inevitable that Gianluigi would find his calling in sports. Initially, his dreams took shape in the midfield, where he played with the ambition of a young boy imagining himself the next great outfield player. Yet, fate had other plans. At the tender age of 11, a pivotal moment occurred. Buffon swapped the midfield for the goalpost, a decision that would change not just his life but the future of football. This move was akin to a young artist discovering their true medium; Buffon had found his canvas.

Buffon's professional career began with Parma in 1995, where he quickly established himself as a player of rare talent. At just 17 years old, he stepped onto the field for the senior team, and the footballing world took notice. His performances were not just about skill; they were about poise, a calmness under pressure that belied his years. In his time with Parma, Buffon helped secure the Coppa Italia, UEFA Cup, and Supercoppa Italiana, a trio of triumphs that marked him out as one of Europe's brightest young goalkeepers.

In 2001, the trajectory of Buffon's career took a monumental leap. Juventus, one of Italy's most storied clubs, came calling with a record-breaking €52 million transfer fee. It was a sum that spoke volumes about the faith they had in Buffon, and he did not disappoint. At Juventus, Buffon didn't just play; he dominated. His presence between the posts was like a fortress, impenetrable and steadfast. Under his watchful eye, Juventus amassed a treasure trove of Serie A titles, Coppa Italia victories, and Supercoppa Italiana wins. Each season was a masterclass in goalkeeping, with Buffon showcasing not just agility and reflexes but an ability to read the game like few others.

Buffon's influence wasn't confined to club football. On the international stage, he was a colossus. He earned his first cap for Italy in 1997, and it wasn't long before he became the cornerstone of the national team. The pinnacle of his international career came in 2006 when Italy lifted the World Cup in Germany. The final, a tense affair against France, saw Buffon pull off a series of saves that were as crucial as they were spectacular. It was in these moments that Buffon's legacy was cemented, his name etched into the annals of football history. His efforts earned him the Lev Yashin Award as the tournament's best goalkeeper, a fitting tribute to a player at the peak of his powers.

However, Buffon's story isn't just one of success. It's also about loyalty, commitment, and the willingness to stand by one's principles. In 2006, the Calciopoli scandal rocked Italian football, leading to Juventus's relegation to Serie B. It was a moment that could have seen Buffon jump ship, with top European clubs eager to snap him up. Yet, Buffon stayed put, a decision that spoke volumes about his character. In an era where loyalty in football can often seem like a relic of the past, Buffon's choice to remain with Juventus endeared him even more to fans and solidified his status as a club legend.

Buffon's career has been defined by its remarkable longevity, a rare quality in the fast-paced world of professional sports. After leaving Juventus in 2018, many thought the curtain was about to fall on his illustrious career. But Buffon had other ideas. He spent a season with Paris Saint-Germain, adding Ligue 1 and Trophée des Champions titles to his already impressive list of accomplishments. In 2019, Buffon returned to Juventus, not as a mere veteran winding down his career but as a leader, a guiding figure for the next generation. And then, in 2021, Buffon made a return to where it all began—Parma. It was a full-circle moment, one that underscored his enduring love for the game.

Off the pitch, Buffon is a figure of humility and intelligence, traits that have won him admirers far beyond the world of football. He has used his platform to champion charitable causes and has been a vocal advocate for fair play. His autobiography, "Numero 1," offers readers an unvarnished look at his life, providing insights into the man behind the gloves. It's a story not just of success but of perseverance, struggle, and the relentless pursuit of excellence.

Buffon's contributions to football have not gone unnoticed. His trophy cabinet is brimming with accolades, including being named Best FIFA Goalkeeper and winning the UEFA Club Goalkeeper of the Year multiple times. His records for the most clean sheets in Serie A and the most appearances for the Italian national team are a testament to his consistent excellence. But beyond the statistics and the silverware, Buffon's legacy is one of inspiration. He has shown that with talent, hard work, and an unyielding passion for one's craft, it is possible to achieve greatness.

In conclusion, Gianluigi Buffon's career is a story of extraordinary skill, unwavering loyalty, and a deep love for the game of football. From his early days as a young boy with big dreams in Carrara to his status as a global icon, Buffon has remained true to himself and to the sport he loves. His exceptional shot-stopping ability, leadership, and dedication to club and country have left an indelible mark on football, inspiring countless young goalkeepers to follow in his footsteps. As the final whistle of his career approaches, Buffon's legacy will continue to resonate, a testament to the heights that can be reached when talent is matched with hard work and a passion that burns as brightly as ever.

The Attributes That Defined Buffon:

- Exceptional shot-stopping ability

- Leadership and composure

- Loyalty and dedication to club and country

Bonus #4:

Hope you've enjoyed this book so far. Think you're an expert on these players now? Think again. How about you test yourself out with a quiz on these players? Just scan the QR code to get your quiz for free.

How to Become the Best of the Best

The BBC's Match of the Day program is the most famous, and certainly the longest running, TV soccer show on earth. Desperate to fill airtime during the pandemic, particularly before soccer returned in front of empty stadiums, the program issued some podcasts and shows in which pundits picked their top tens. You know the sort of thing. Top ten goals, top ten Premier League strikers, top ten FA Cup goals. All rather parochial. Sadly, they have yet to come up with their top ten greatest players.

Even creating such a list is a dubious activity. The first and last of our greats apart, perhaps, an argument could be made to supplant every one of the players we have chosen with another. Actually, ranking them in some sort of order is more controversial still.

So here we go.

Tenth: George Best - It was not the Irishman's fault that he was born in a tiny nation and therefore never even went to a World Cup, let alone have the chance of winning it. Further, something in Best's personality saw him destroy his own career, then his own life. Both were cut tragically short. None of that, though, should detract from his genius on the pitch. If soccer is about entertainment more than anything else – and perhaps it should be – then Best would appear higher up our order. But it is also about winning. And for that reason, we have to place him here. Last, yes, but last among greats.

Ninth: Peter Schmeichel – The goalkeepers' union will be delighted that a keeper makes the top ten. There might be more debate over whether that keeper should be Peter Schmeichel. But the giant Dane was also a giant of the game, and (along with Eric Cantona, another who could well have made this list, in the outfield department) was possibly the single most important player during Manchester United's era of near dominance under Sir Alex Ferguson. Further, in helping the minnows of Denmark to lift the European Championship, he has an achievement worthy of inclusion in any list of soccer's most remarkable achievements.

Eighth: **Johan Cruyff** - Had the Dutch lifted the 1974 World Cup, as they should have done; had Cruyff not been subject to very real death threats in 1978 and provided the extra element to give them the trophy in that year's competition, then 'El Salvador' (the Savior) would also have featured higher in the final positions. As great a player as he was, for Cruyff perhaps it was his legacy to the game that has been his most important contribution.

Along, of course, with the Cruyff turn. Which supporter does not leap to the air with joy when they see their own soccer hero emulate the brilliant Dutchman with that little touch of skill?

Seventh: Zinedine Zidane – To overcome the challenges that Zidane beat as a child and youth merits huge admiration. To possess the skill, technique and vision with which Zidane was blessed is equally remarkable. The French national side of Zidane's era was the finest in the world, and Zidane was its finest player.

Sixth: Cristiano Ronaldo – Still a world beating goal scorer at the age of thirty-six, who knows how long the great man can continue? Ronaldo epitomizes the thinking soccer player. One who has adapted his game with time and circumstances. One who will, surely, become a great manager one day.

Fifth: Lionel Messi - To be blessed with two such greats at the same time, to witness them at their peak in the same league. Lucky Spain. To do so at a time when soccer is more popular than it has ever been. And when it is available in more homes to more people than ever before. What a delight. Many, especially younger, fans would rate Ronaldo and Messi, or Messi and Ronaldo, as the greatest ever. Maybe in time that will prove to be the case. Some perspective is needed to reach such a conclusion. Each is remarkable in their own way. We believe that Messi, with his stronger all-round game, marginally tips the scales in his favor as the greatest player of the current century. It is easy enough to make the case the other way.

Fourth: Bobby Moore - Maybe it is his very limitations that push Moore so high up this list. Whilst every other player had already been marked for potential greatness by their mid-teens, Moore was still debating whether he even wanted to be a footballer. Yet, if hard work, dedication and making the most of your talents are signs of being the best, Moore had them in abundance. As do the others on this list. Yet of them all, Moore was possibly the greatest captain among a list of great captains. As fine a player as he was, as brilliantly as he could read a game, it was what Moore brought to the players around him, as much as what he offered himself, that makes him stand out. Plus, England is both the birthplace of soccer and, as a populous nation which worships the game as much as any other, one of its relatively least successful. At least in terms of winning major trophies. That the one title to date came under Bobby Moore's leadership cannot be ignored.

Third: Ferenc Puskas – Most readers of this book will not be old enough to have seen Ferenc Puskas play. Or the Magical Magyars. There is little in the way of clips of his genius available. Still, we can enjoy the poor-quality footage and marvel at a man who secured two wonderful careers, separated as they were by the incursion of Soviet communism. Puskas did not have the build of a soccer player; he was not blessed with outstanding speed (although, he was quick enough) but he was a striker who scored so many goals. Watching clips, it becomes apparent that he achieved this with superb technique. When Puskas shot, it was low, it was hard, and it was accurate. Soccer is about scoring goals, more than anything else. Puskas was the best of all time at doing this.

Second: Diego Maradona – How can a man so flawed be one so great? The best dribbler of all time, the most balanced maestro in the history of the game. A God to many, a genius to all. If Shakespeare were writing today, Diego Maradona would be his next great tragic hero. If Diego Maradona's life proved anything, it is that soccer can change lives. Maybe sport is about more than what happens on the pitch.

First: Pele – Pele was the perfect footballer and remains the perfect ambassador of the game. The greatest player of the greatest team of all time. A man who eschewed such accolade but possessed genius in buckets. Time can diminish a reputation. It should never diminish his.

Ranking these players has been a bit of fun. Few will agree with the order. Other cases can be made. And should be. Of more import is identifying the factors which made these players great. Of course, each was possessed with astonishing natural skill, with innate athleticism. But each experienced other factors beyond the physical. Mental attributes, social conditions and environmental factors which should seemingly play little in their rise to the top, but which have done so. Ten soccer greats is not a definitive number from which to draw conclusions, although it is enough to throw up theories, to suggest hypotheses to help identify future greats, to see which youngsters currently playing in academies, or even in the streets of run down, impoverished communities, might not just break into the professional game, play for their country, win trophies but one day stand beside the players in this book.

It should be stated that in choosing these players, we considered only their talents, their achievements and their legacies to the game.

There was no attempt to find players who shared other characteristics. We started with the players and their soccer abilities and careers, and then sought to study their past, and especially their upbringings.

Yet the overwhelming factor to emerge is that these players came from humble, impoverished backgrounds. Peter Schmeichel apart. Then, as we have said, keepers are different. That level of impoverishment did vary from player to player. The British contingent were working class, but not destitute. Perhaps that reflects British society as much as British soccer players. Yet at the other extreme, the likes of Ronaldo, of Pele, Zidane and of Maradona grew up in abject poverty. Ferenc Puskas learned the game juggling packed rags instead of a football. Economic poverty, at least. Messi's family lacked any degree of financial comfort, despite the sacrifices made by his parents to pay for the drugs he needed to grow. Cruyff, like Moore and Best, was firmly working class even if he enjoyed an acceptable standard of living.

What can we conclude from this? That the poverty the players experienced drove them on to escape the life they were living? Maybe. Whilst not every person from a poor background has the drive – or the opportunity – to leave it behind, perhaps it was the case that for these

168

sporting greats circumstances came together to give them the opportunity – the impetus - to fight their way out of poverty.

What is too simplistic is to conclude that the majority of our players came from a poor background because soccer players come from a poor background, as a rule. As we showed earlier, soccer has its roots in the playing fields of English public schools, well before it became the entertainment for factory workers in Victorian Britain. A study reported in 2019 looked at the educational background of top sports players in the UK. It was the sort of study which really could only take place in the UK, since that is one of the few countries in the world with a highly established and prominent independent educational system. About 8-10% of young people are educated at fee paying schools in the UK. Perhaps it is not surprising that a third of cricketers and rugby players came from such establishments. After all, many maintained schools (those run by the state) do not have the facilities or expertise to coach cricket, and rugby is not widely played, certainly at primary level, because of lack of training of staff and health and safety concerns. These two sports tend to be found in the private sector when it comes to school sports at least. (Interestingly, the figure for female players of these sports coming from independent schools is much lower, perhaps indicating how the segregation in terms of sports played sits along gender lines in the independent sector.) However, five per cent of all professional UK soccer players are privately educated. Given that many independent schools do not play soccer (it was a higher figure in the days when today's professionals were of school age because the concerns over rugby are beginning to infiltrate even the hotbeds of the sport), that figure is not statistically significant.

Yet perhaps something of more significance comes when we look at the family support our soccer greats received in their formative years. It is exclusively encouraging and supportive. Again, that is not a surprise. No doubt were we looking at great musicians, or great athletes, or scientists or writers that element of parental support would be present. Every one of the ten players we have considered here came from a home where their parents actively supported their enthusiasm for sport.

Similarly, each one of these players had considerable exposure to a mentor from an early age. The older players, such as Pele and Puskas, had top performing soccer players as parents. It is an interesting concept to note that the more recent players would, had their parents been top professional sports players, not have grown up in poverty. In recent times success in professional sport has equated to wealth. Peter Schmeichel, of course, is the father of the current Danish goalkeeper, Kasper. But then, as we keep saying, keepers are different. It is also worth noting the sacrifices our players' parents made to give their sons the best chance of making it and escaping poverty. Maradona and Messi's parents in particular. Zidane's parents too, paying for coaching they really could not afford. Messi and Zidane's wider families made huge commitments to support their siblings; in Messi's case even travelling to Spain in support of their brother's ambitions. We also see the role of mothers acting often as a mitigating influence, helping to keep their sons grounded, and stressing the importance of education. When we hear of so many talented youngsters failing to make the grade, we might conclude that it is this very determination to keep their son living in the real world that makes their parents so important in their progress towards fame and fortune.

Maybe there is some significance in the fact that, for whatever reasons (the wish for personal gain, commitment to work to keep the family above water or just ignorance) the two sets of parents who seemed to least support their child as they grew older, Maradona and Best's parents, produced the children who most went off the rails. That is not to criticize these parents, who still sought to do their best for their children.

Puskas and Cruyff grew up in the shadow of their local soccer stadiums, which undoubtedly influenced their love of the sport, and another common theme is the love for the game these players formed from a very young age. In all cases, a coach spotted them young, and oversaw their development. These early coaches were, in every case, committed fully to their charges, further helping them to escape the poverty into which they were born. Even if Maradona's mentor may have acted in a dubious way to allow his charge's goals to be reached.

Mental fortitude also seems to be a very significant attribute among these great players. Notice the common thread of a major setback hitting them early in life. It could be physical ones, such as with Zidane, Messi and Maradona. Emotional ones such as with Cruyff, with his father passing so young, or George Best, who lost the grandfather he adored at just eleven years of age. It is interesting to note, also, that Moore always believed he was not good enough to play the game at a high level, an opinion seemingly ratified by the scouts who saw him as a boy. It could be other emotional frustrations, such as with Ronaldo at school, or again Moore and Best with their unhappiness during their education. Maradona and Zidane too had little time for schooling. Pele, perhaps alone among the group, was bullied because of his lisp, although the discrimination Maradona faced because of his cultural and indigenous background was also deeply prejudicial.

Often, these players overcame bad fortune during their careers – Ronaldo losing his father when he was about to break into Sporting's first team; Moore being arrested on false charges, Ronaldo again facing the horror of being accused of rape, Messi and his taxation problems, Best and his homesickness, then becoming the playboy favourite, before playboy victim, of the media. Puskas seeing his homeland ravaged by invading Soviet forces.

It is true that many people, from all walks of life, undergo trauma and setback. What each of the players here seemed to manage was to overcome their misfortune quickly, and without it impacting their focus and commitment. The one exception to this rule being, perhaps, George Best.

Another interesting fact is that many of these players were small as youngsters. Lots were late developers. Frequently, first reports suggested that they were too small, too light or too frail to make it in the game. Did that very vulnerability play a part in their rise? Maybe it did. As smaller players they could not dominate through their physical prowess, even if they were very quick. Instead, their ability to become leading players in their boys' teams came from outstanding technique – one which would stand up to scrutiny as they moved up the levels. It came from the perfection of existing skills and the acquisition of new ones. Frequently, these players became properly two footed, because they needed every advantage on the field.

The wish to be the best is a common enough one, at any level. Yet as youngsters, these boys hard to work hard to achieve their goals. They could not be the strongest player simply because they were bigger than their opponents, could kick the ball further or harder, or use their long legs to run more quickly because these were attributes they did not possess. They had to practice and practice to become as good as they wanted to be. That hunger was established as a youngster and stayed with them throughout their careers, again, possibly, George Best apart.

Further, being small they had a greater agility, could twist and turn to avoid the risk of impact injury. In short, the very slightness of their stature helped them to turn into the players they would become. Both physically, and mentally.

Luck inevitably played a role in these players' development. The luck to be spotted, which seems a common theme, the luck to be picked to play at just the right time, as with Zidane. The good fortune to be playing the game when a keen and influential person saw them. Without that good fortune, maybe neither Puskas nor Maradona would have achieved the status that they did.

Linked to good luck is fortune with timing. Would Pele have made it had he not grown up just at the moment that indoor soccer was developing in Brazil, allowing him to develop his incredible skills to such a level? Hopefully yes, but who could say for sure? Or had Puskas and Cruyff not been the right age just when their respective first clubs were regenerating their youth programs, would they too have missed out?

So maybe among these conclusions, observations and questions we can find the strongest formula for creating the soccer superstars of tomorrow. Challenges – economic, social and personal – which the player is determined to overcome. A properly supportive family to take the player through those initial stages before a new mentor can step in. That mentor often a coach, sometimes a teacher or parent. The good fortune to be in the right place at the right time to be spotted and to get the chance to perform. Again and again, these players were young when they made their breakthrough. Perhaps that is not so surprising, after all, even as mid-teens they were good enough to make the grade and had they not been playing for a coach ready to give youth its head, they probably would not have achieved all that they were able to do.

Back to determination, fortitude, the will to win – whatever we wish to call it. These players are ones who practiced for hours a day as a child, who used the time between playing to perfect their skills and hone their technique. But they never lost that will power, once they had tasted success as a young player, they wanted it again and again.

These were players who also represented the biggest clubs, and therefore performed alongside the best players. Even Bobby Moore, who spent most of the best years of his career with West Ham United, not the biggest team in Europe, or England or even London. But he was there at a time West Ham were blossoming into one of the most attractive teams in the country. Timing, again. But equally, whilst these players did benefit from all the advantages of a top club, and being surrounded by the best teammates, coaches and infrastructure, they did so because they were the best themselves. A case of both the chicken and the egg coming first.

But the biggest ingredient of all, the one which cannot be taught, is pure talent. Athletic talent. The ability to read a game, to be in the right place at the right time more often than both their teammates and their opponents, and to have the exceptional skill and the secure technique to utilize opportunities when they come along. To create those opportunities themselves if they did not arrive courtesy of their teammates.

Yes, we can see that every one of the players we have considered in this book received support and mentorship, but the biggest advantages they received came from themselves – their own hard work, their own mental strength, and their own unsurpassable soccer talents.

There are excellent biographies and autobiographies available about each of our greats. Here is a recommended book about each of the players, to satisfy questions this anthology has not had the scope to answer and to further readers' knowledge about each player.

1. Pele by Pele.
2. Ferenc Puskas, Captain of Hungary by Ferenc Puskas.
3. My Turn, the Autobiography by Johan Cruyff
4. Messi vs Ronaldo: the greatest rivalry by Luca Caiola.
5. Schmeichel – the Autobiography by Peter Schmeichel with Egon Balsby.
6. Bobby Moore the definitive biography by Jeff Powell.
7. Best – an intimate biography by Michael Parkinson
8. Zidane by Patrick Fort
9. Maradona - The Hand of God by Jimmy Burns

178

The end... almost!

Reviews are not easy to come by.

As an independent author with a tiny marketing budget, I rely on readers, like you, to leave a short review on Amazon.

Even if it's just a sentence or two!

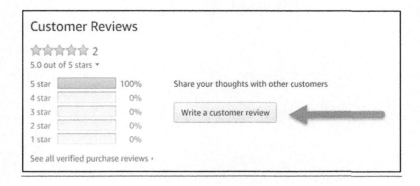

So if you enjoyed the book, please...

Thank you from the bottom of my heart for purchasing this book and reading it to the end.

Made in the USA
Las Vegas, NV
14 December 2024

14170245R00105